Also by Elick Moll

The Perilous Spring of
Morris Seidman

ELICK MOLL

The Perilous Spring of Morris Seidman

HOUGHTON MIFFLIN COMPANY BOSTON

1972

FIRST PRINTING C

ISBN: 0-395-13949-X
LIBRARY OF CONGRESS CATALOG CARD NUMBER: 72-1106
PRINTED IN THE UNITED STATES
OF AMERICA

For all the Vangies

The Perilous Spring of
Morris Seidman

I

Greetings, come in, *bien venido,* it's been a long time, I'm very glad to see you. *Siéntese* . . . You guessed it. My wife and I just got back from a trip to Spain. I could just as well have said welcome, sit down but what's the use of traveling if you can't get a little return on the investment? And who better could I show off that I'm becoming a regular linguist, if not to my writer friend?

So tell me, what's with you, *mi amigo.* I figured it's about time I should be seeing you. Even though you got to hate New York, you have to come sometimes to see a show on Broadway, an opera or a ballet in Lincoln Center, to take another look at the Frick Museum — they couldn't destroy the city entirely. We've even got our own *corrida,* you could join in every night at theater time, with the taxis charging down the streets and the people yelling and chasing them — who needs Pamplona? Well, I'm glad I'm still on your list of what to see when you visit the Metropolis. One of the attractions, or maybe I should say, curiosities. Like the Flatiron building. I think they are considering to tear me down soon, also.

No, not depressed exactly. But I am semi-retired you know. Like semi-pregnant. Or semi-starving. What it means, my friend, is that I haven't got the courage, or maybe the honesty to say simply: finished, period, end of the line. It was entirely my own idea, you understand, something *I*

1

wanted, not anybody else. Still and all — I tell you, we're peculiar animals, human beings. I'm glad — glad? I'm tickled to death not to have any more the responsibility and the headaches and the complaints from the shop foreman and the conferences with the union delegate — and yet, the same time, I feel kind of — pushed out. With an honorary degree. Senior Citizen.

Anyway, I turned over the business to my son Harold to run. He is very good at it. Also he is polite, considerate, makes a point to consult me about everything. I think he takes from a psychiatrist every week, how to handle the old man who's still got a 51 percent interest in the partnership, and a veto power, and could make a mishmash of everything if he is not properly sedated with a compliment every two hours. But I've still got time to feel pretty useless.

Oh, sure, I occupy myself. Listen, how many years was I dreaming about the time when I could divorce myself from this business, let go of it already and it should let go of me, and I would have finally leisure for the music I wanted to hear, the museums I wanted to visit, the books I wanted to read, the places I wanted to see. But now, an ironic thing. When it's a dream, these things, you've never got enough time for them. When you've got to make a life from them, it's a whole different story.

Golf? Listen, if you are a friend of mine, please don't talk to me about golf. This is one thing I didn't dream about in the old days. Never fell into my head. I couldn't see the attraction, standing over a ball, giving it a *hock,* then walking a block to give it another *hock.* But now that I am a member of an expensive club in Westchester, and I've been playing for a year, I really got to hate it. I hate everything about it, the pro, the lessons, the locker room, the jokes,

2

grown men, grandfathers, with the scores and the stances and the strokes — and Harold and Sophie are always pushing me to go and play golf. "It's good for me."

Another thing that's good for me is long walks. Explain me something. In Rome, or Paris, or London, I could walk all day long and in the evening, after dinner, the best thing I could think of to do for recreation, is to take a walk. And I don't get tired. Here in New York, if I've got a call to make, or an errand to do ten blocks away, I have to get my car and get furious with the traffic, or try to take a taxi and stand wishing all good things for her future to the lady with packages who gives me such a shove away, just as I got my hand on the door, that I'll have a sore kidney for a week afterward.

But I better stop with this talk or we'll be discussing why I don't move away from this impossible city. I've thought about it, more than once. Actually, there's no good reason. Except one. This is home.

I'll tell you, my friend, one thing and another, even if it's not by request, it's not so easy to retire. You'll see yourself, when the time comes. Except, I suppose, with a writer it's different. You are semi-retired all the time. You could *draydle* around doing nothing, you don't have to explain to people why. You are — what is the expression when a farmer gives a piece of ground a chance to rest — yes, lying fallow. In TV, I understand, some of the writers could turn out scripts and lie fallow at the same time.

Well, I'm joking, you understand. I know what a tough job it is, writing. Even if it's not Shakespeare, or Hemingway. I tried a couple of times lately to get some of my ideas put down on paper, you know, experiences while traveling, impressions — I got a new respect for people who could make a living, doing this.

It's a peculiar thing, with me. When it's conversation, like now, seems to me I talk like everybody else. Only three times as much, of course. But when I start to write down the same thing on paper, suddenly I'm a foreigner. It's like someone is looking over my shoulder and saying that the verb is not in the right place, or you're not supposed to start a sentence with So, or you're supposed to say As, not Like, and so on, and finally I say to myself who needs it, I'm not a schoolboy, and I give up.

Still, if you keep your threat to stop coming to New York — and I wouldn't blame you — maybe it will come to a point where writing is the only way I could communicate — God, how I got to hate this word, it's drummed into your head from morning to night in the magazines, on the radio, on television, usually together with the word "failure" — failure to communicate — the other day, I looked up in the thesaurus you gave me, to see maybe there's a substitute, you could usually find at least a dozen different words to say something but for this miserable word there's really nothing else. You don't want to say "have intercourse with," people would think you've got something else in mind entirely. But I hope it wouldn't come to this, the only way I could have intercourse with you is by mail. I would miss your visits very much, I always keep thinking, especially now I've got so much time on my hands, *this* I've got to tell to my writer friend.

And speaking of time on my hands, there's enough now so I could mix into other people's business. Recently I got into a thing with my nephew Ralphie, my sister Bessie's boy — but look here, I'm doing all the talking, tell me better what's going on with you in Hollywood now. I have to apologize to you I didn't get a chance to look at the series you are doing for television. Somehow that title — "Frankie and Jennie" — my finger gets paralyzed on the clicker . . . You

4

too? I'm relieved to hear it. You got it in your contract you don't have to watch, only write? Good for you. So you could just take the royalty and go to the movies, right? Okay, then I don't have to excuse myself. We understand each other.

Ralphie? Sure I'll tell you, if you want, why should I start after all these years being circumspect about my family. (It's a new word I picked up, I'm glad I got a chance to use it on you.) Actually, there's not much to tell, unless to be a young man twenty years old in these days is already a story all by itself. I've got to admit Ralphie is a little special, even for today. Precocious. Once upon a time if a boy was precocious he started to write poetry when he was seven, or play the piano or recite from the classics. Ralphie's precocious was different. He started having dates with girls when he was seven. When he was nine he went into the hubcap business. And so on. You think you've got the picture? I'll confuse you a little. This boy has got an IQ of one hundred and sixty and a steady average in college of C minus. His sexual IQ, I don't think they've got a computer for it yet. He's six feet two, looks like a choir boy, if you could imagine a Jewish choir boy, with a beard; so far the army doesn't want him because he shows up too unstable on the examinations. I guess they're afraid if they gave him a gun he would start shooting the generals. He's got a burning sense of injustice, don't ask me to tell you against what, but he's got it.

And it's a very special thing, this sense of injustice. It gives you the right to march around a school and stop other students from getting in, or to lock up a professor in his laboratory for a day without food, or to burn up papers that is his lifetime's work and has maybe got something in it to contribute to the world, improve it a little — and doing these things you don't have to worry that you are being unjust to someone else. You've got a license from God, or from Mao

5

Tse-tung, which is more or less the same thing, to knock down everything and remake the world, what it will be like afterward, a prison camp, an ant hill, doesn't matter, anything you do to accomplish this is okay.

Well, I've been hearing about this boy, you understand, one thing and another, for a long time. My sister Bessie doesn't keep any secrets from me. Frankly, I wish she would keep a couple but my misfortune is I got her complete confidence. About a month ago she calls me up and this is how the conversation goes. More or less.

"Morris," she said, "I've come to the end. I got no place to turn. The only thing I can do is kill myself."

"So what are you calling me for," I say. "You want an advice how?"

This sounds maybe tough but I've been dealing with this woman a lifetime and I learned long ago there is only one way to handle her.

"I suppose," she says, "if I *would* kill myself it would be a relief for you. You wouldn't have to take five minutes off from doing nothing to talk to me."

"Bessie," I said, "I'm not one bit worried that you'll kill yourself. Not as long as you've got a telephone and you can call me up every day to give me a conniption."

"Wait," she says. "One day you'll be sorry — they'll break in the door and find me stretched out, dead — "

"Do me a favor," I say. "If you should decide finally, don't wear the blue satin I made for you last year. Harold is going to feature it again in the line this season."

So she can't help herself, she has to laugh but just for a second, like a gargle. "Some brother I got," she says. "Morris Seidman. A pillow in the community. Everybody could come to you and lay down with their troubles. But for your own sister — a stone. No feelings, no heart — "

6

"All right, Bessie," I say. "That's enough. You got something to say to me, say it. Otherwise I'm going to hang up. What's the use being semi-retired if I have to be on the phone all day."

"It's Ralphie," she says. "He will put me in my grave."

Well, Ralphie. I haven't kept up entirely with his activities the past few years, this is not Bessie's fault, but I've been away a good deal, we made a trip around the world, as you know, and lately this Mediterranean tour — so now comes some pictures of Ralphie going through my mind, possibilities. Marching, sitting in, sitting out, socking policemen, taking LSD, maybe he's in Bellevue, in jail —

"You know what this boy done to me?" Bessie says.

"Only to you?" I say. "Where's Myron?"

"Where's Myron. If he was a father instead of a pinochle player, maybe Ralphie would be a boy like other boys."

"Which other boys?" I ask her. "The ones I hear about, your Ralphie is a paragon."

"My Ralphie is a bum," she says. "And I don't want to hear any excuses for him."

"How can I make excuses for him. I don't know what he's done."

"Nothing. A little nothing. He's got himself mixed up with a topless girl works in a joint in New Jersey."

"Is she Jewish at least?" It's maybe not a brilliant question but *you* figure out what to say, your nephew is mixed up with a topless girl who works in a joint in New Jersey.

"What do I care if she's Jewish," Bessie yells. "She's a bum."

"How did you find out about her?"

"How. He came and told us he's got intentions to marry her."

"When?"

7

"How do I know when? All I got to do is open my mouth to ask a question, he's out the door and halfway to the subway."

"Well, it's possible she's a nice girl. At least she's working, she's not on the streets — "

"I'll ask you a question, my fine brother. If your Harold would have come to you eight years ago and said he's going to marry a girl who makes a good living serving drinks in a joint, dressed in half a pair of tights and pushing her bust in the customers' faces, and who knows what she does afterward, you would have been dancing with joy, ha?"

Well, she's got a point. But I reminded her. "You remember I had a problem with Sophie when Harold told us he was going to marry a Gentile girl, a model in the shop. Not topless. Semi-topless. Sophie was convinced it would be a disaster. So they got married and now we've got a grandchild who asks questions about Jewish history that I can't answer and Harold is a fine, settled young man, runs the business better than I ever did, and Sophie wouldn't trade you our daughter-in-law for any dozen girls you could pick out from the Hadassah."

"What kind of comparison are you making?" she said. "Ralphie is twenty years old, he's got two more years to finish college, three more legal . . ."

I didn't want to tell her the way I figure, Ralphie has got at least four more years to finish college, or anyway get kicked out finally, and forget about the legal. But you understand me, I don't want to be cruel to my sister. I love her in my own way and she is really not a stupid woman, at bottom. Only after forty years you get a little tired, digging. You know what I mean?

"What can I do, Bessie," I say to her. "This kind of a problem — it's got to work itself out — "

8

"You are his uncle. Have a talk with him. Maybe you'll have some influence — "

"All right, Bessie," I say. "I'll look into the situation, all what I could do. But don't get your hopes up. These kids today, looks to me they figure the worst enemy they got is the older generation. Except for two minutes a week, when they are reaching for their allowance."

Well, she gives me the name of the girl, Vangie Jamison, and the place where she is working, the Gay Blades Club in Weehawken. So where do I start? If I call in Ralphie for a talk, I know what will happen. I had it with my own Harold. Maybe not exactly the same. Looking back now, doesn't seem to me Harold was so wrong. He had his reasons to complain about my attitude. I could have been more understanding, no question. But this new crop of young people, I don't know where the understanding starts. It's like they would be talking nuclear equations and I'm stuck with simple arithmetic. I lost touch with them completely. I don't have the least idea what goes on in their minds. I listened to this man Leary on the television, a couple years ago, you know the LSD fellow, I understand he's some kind of a god with the college kids, and I thought I was losing my mind. It's like fifty years ago, a professor from a reputable school would advise you to get drunk every night because this will expand your mental horizon. If you work at it real hard you will get to see technicolor snakes and baboons and this will explain to you the riddle of the universe.

I got a pretty good idea how it will go if I try to tell Ralphie what to do with his life, he should wait a while before he takes a big step like marriage, what about finishing up with school first, after all from what is he going to support a wife now, and maybe children — he will give me a short speech to mind my own business, tell me I did enough harm

9

in the world already without starting on him now; there'll be a few words thrown in about the Establishment, the Power Structure, he'll ask me how much profit I'm making out of the Vietnam war and the tenement houses I don't own in Harlem — and if I got the nerve to tell him it's not exactly a glorious idea for his family that he should get married to a topless girl who works in a joint, he's liable to spit in my eye and break up the furniture altogether.

I'm thinking about the situation, trying to figure out how I could attack it, when our star salesman, Larry Kogen, comes in. You think he's maybe changed a little since you wrote about him in the book? After all, it's quite a few years. Maybe he settled down, got married or something? Nothing. The same Larry. Maybe he made a few improvements in his apartment. Like perfume comes out of the heat register now and you could change the lighting with your foot instead of having to reach for a switch and maybe he's got a file cabinet now instead of the black book. Otherwise, the same routine. Girls and girls. I decided something. People don't change. They only get older.

"What's the matter, boss?" he asks. "You look unhappy."

"I'm semi-retired," I said. "How else should I look?"

"Why don't you go out to the club, play some golf?"

"Listen, Larry, couldn't you think of something else I could do sometime. Besides golf?"

"I could think of something," he says. "Good, wholesome, indoor exercise. I'll give you the key to my apartment. Won't cost you any more than the greens fee — "

"Thank you very much. I got a nephew who handles this department for the family." And I tell him about the new problem with Ralphie.

I get a typical Larry reaction. "The kid's twenty years old. He's having a fling. What's the big commotion?"

"What fling?" I said. "This boy flang himself out of his

10

crib and he's been flinging ever since. The commotion is he wants to marry this girl. And the next fling is into the divorce court. Where else could it go, with a girl like this?"

"Where does she work?"

"Some place in New Jersey. The Gay Blades Club."

"You want me to go out there with you, look the situation over?"

"What good will it do? If she's got her hooks into the boy — "

"There's a couple of possibilities. Maybe scare her off. Maybe some money. Or maybe, if she's not a dog, I'll move in and take her over for a while. Shake Ralphie loose." He gives his tie a little straighten; funny how much a person could tell about himself with such a little movement.

"What if we run into Ralphie there?" I say.

"You can put it on me. We're casing the joint for a customer or something."

"It's a club," I said. "You need a membership, no?"

"Yeah. They screen you. You've got to swear not to order a pink lady or a sloe gin fizz. And if the twenty dollar bill you give the head waiter turns out to be handmade your membership is canceled."

"I don't know," I said. "Is this the right thing to do? The boy must be in love — "

"Okay, you want him to marry a tramp, forget it. I'm just offering to lend a hand."

Well, for Larry, I know this is a figure of speech. But whatever he's offering to lend, I got to appreciate it. After all it's my sister's boy and I *don't* want he should marry a tramp.

"I'll call home," I said, "and say I wouldn't be for dinner."

When I got Sophie on the phone I didn't want to tell her the whole business about Ralphie so I just said I was staying down to eat with Larry.

"You don't get enough of him in the shop?" she says.

11

"You've been telling me to get out more," I said, "not sit around the house evenings, and mope — "

"So with Larry you'll sit around in a restaurant and mope."

"You got a better suggestion? Your Dr. Bernstein from the club? I'll sit and listen all night to a lecture on psychoanalysis?"

"All right, Morris," she says. "Have a good dinner. Enjoy yourself. And don't forget to take your enzymes afterward."

"I know what's bothering you," I said. "You figure with Larry, there's got to be girls."

"It never occurred to me, Morris, but if this is what you think you need, you have my blessing."

"Could I have it in writing?"

"You don't want it in writing. You want me to say 'don't you dare.'"

"So why don't you? Because you don't think it's possible I should have a thing with a girl. I'm too old, too decrepit — "

"Morris," she says, "why don't you stop fighting the idea and go have a few sessions with an analyst."

"Oh, for heaven's sake, you're going to start with the analyst business again? On the phone yet?"

"Don't get excited," she says, "this is your loving wife, remember? I don't like this mood you are sinking into lately. You put a label on yourself, semi-retired, and it's like you want everybody to think you became an old man overnight. To me you are still an attractive, exciting, vigorous man. I want *you* to think of yourself the same way."

"Thank you," I said. "When I get home, if I'm not too tired, we'll sit up and watch the late show on television. Vigorously."

Well, I am not a writer so I wouldn't try to describe you the Gay Blades Club. But I could tell you my reaction. Some blades. The average age is maybe fifty-five and be-

12

lieve me they are not the type to wear a lace jabot around
the neck and a handkerchief in the sleeve. And if they are
gay, I'm Peter Pan. They sit there, crowded in at the little
tables, drunk, half drunk or trying to be drunk, a three-piece
band is making enough noise for twelve, sometimes a girl
comes out to sing, like pouring hot oil in your ear, and the
waitresses are walking around, all colors and sizes, except
the bust, this is at least thirty-eight, because it's a require-
ment of the management, I suppose. All of them are young,
kids actually, but already with that hard, empty look in the
eyes, no more surprises waiting, no more mystery — I'm
telling you it's so sad, I couldn't express to you how sad it
makes me feel.

I've got to explain myself. The furthest thing from my
mind is that there is something not right or not decent
about a woman who is naked, or half naked. (I'm not talking
about those size forty-eights in Miami Beach, with their
bikinis, this is another story. Got nothing to do with decency. It's a question of social responsibility. If you are
a woman who's been a pig all your life and at fifty you're
eight sizes too big, especially around the middle, this should
be a private thing between you and your husband or your
psychiatrist. For the rest, cover yourself up at least and don't
spoil the scenery and everybody's appetite.)

But nudity. I remember an afternoon in Madrid, in the
Prado, there was a picture by Goya, you know the famous
one of that naked Countess and I stood there looking, I don't
know how long, Sophie had to pull me away, finally. It
wasn't only a painting I was looking at. A work of art. It
was a woman too. A luscious, sexy woman, to make your
heart beat a little faster. Even if you are semi-retired. But
it's not a feeling that you want to get in bed with her. Maybe
that's part of it, but only part. Something bigger, I don't
know how to express it, except maybe to say it's kind of a

13

religious feeling. I know if I said this to a rabbi he would hit me on the head with the Talmud and tell me to go wash out my mind with soap. But I'm serious. Religious is the only word I could think of. You are grateful to someone, something, for being alive, for being a man, to know what it is to have a woman in bed, the fantastic thing, never gets stale, not like Tchaikovsky's Piano Concerto, say, but always the same power, like it would be the first time. Seems to me this is some kind of a miracle, what happens between a man and a woman. And here is a Goya, a genius, he's saying all this in a picture.

And then there is this Gay Blades Club and seems to me it's a shame, a sin against nature. Not morality. I don't want to be a judge, what's moral and what's not. Let everybody do what they want, so long as they are not hurting anybody else. But for me the crime is that they are peeing on life, these people, all these promoters of the topless girls, the strippers, the advertisers, the TV people. They are saying, this marvel, this mystery of the sexes, it's only merchandise to make a profit, to sell deodorants, or mouthwash, or hair oil or whatever.

Well, I don't want to give a lecture. Maybe the way things were when I grew up made a lot of problems for people. Maybe the young people today don't have these problems. So they've got other problems. They've got to take marijuana or LSD to find out what we knew about life from kissing a girl in a hallway.

A girl goes by our table, long blond hair to the shoulders; she's wearing red silk tights, with net stockings the same color and a big bow in back, looks like a bustle, and she's carrying a tray. "Cigars, cigarettes," she says, singsong. I don't know why but I got a memory suddenly from way back on the East Side. *I cash clothes . . . I cash clothes . . . strawberries . . . fresh strawberries . . .* They didn't have

14

what to eat, those peddlers, most of the time; they were dead on their feet from *shlepping* around their baskets of rags or fruit or safety pins or whatever, but they made a kind of song out of it, sad yes, poor yes, but hope too was in it. Maybe tomorrow will be better, or next week, or next year. Maybe there will be one day money for a decent place to live, for an education for the children . . .

But these girls, I understand they make very good money, they are never hungry, they've got "admirers" I suppose and clothes. And they got also their little song, "cigars, cigarettes," and it's got a music in it like sour milk dropping into an empty pail. And when you call them over for a cigar, they got a smile for you, from the empty eyes, and if you've got a dark corner in your heart somewhere, I promise you it wouldn't get any lighter from that smile.

But this doesn't seem to bother Larry, any of this stuff. "That's a pair of knockers for a baronial castle," he says. "I wonder if she's had the paraffin treatment."

"Cigars, cigarettes," the girl sings.

"Thanks, honey. We're looking for Vangie Jamison. Which one is she?"

The girl looks around. "I don't see her."

"But she's here tonight."

"Yes, she's here."

"When you see her, ask her to stop by this table, will you, honey? and take care of those boobs, don't get them caught in a revolving door." She gives him the same smile, a Xerox copy and walks away singing, "Cigars, cigarettes."

"Larry," I said, "explain me something. What kind of a species is it, these gay blades who come here? What is going on that I don't understand, that's supposed to be fun, amusement, excitement, I don't know what. Here are a bunch of men, middle-aged at least, looks like they are businessmen, must be pretty successful I suppose, or they couldn't afford

15

to pay the check, must have some brains, judgment to get where they got — what are they doing here? Waiting for one of these girls to trip so they'll maybe get a nipple in their mouth?"

"Morris, you going to start making a Talmudic *tsimmes* out of this? They're here to have a few drinks and enjoy themselves. What else?"

"But how? What is there here to enjoy? A bunch of girls who should be home in bed with a glass of milk, or studying their lessons, walking around half naked — what does this do for these blades? At least if it was a fancy house and they were picking out a girl to go to bed with, it would be like in a meat market, but I could understand it. But this. Explain it to me. What's the attraction?"

"Do me a favor, Morris," he says. "You came here to find out about this girl, Vangie. All right, we'll find out and beat it. I don't know why, for Christ's sake, every time I make a move with you, it's got to end up as philosophy or a sociology lesson."

A girl comes up to the table now. The bosom is bare like the other one: the costume is a little different, black net tights with a taffeta apron as big as a handkerchief and she's carrying an order book instead of a tray. But especially what is different is the way she carries herself. If *you* wanted to say "like a princess" you would try to think of some other expression, because by now maybe a hundred thousand girls have carried themselves like princesses in books and you don't want the critics to think you are a tired writer. Especially since they got their eye on you now because you are making a fortune in television. But me, a semi-retired dress manufacturer, this is the thought I had watching her and I don't have to strain myself. Except for you to see the picture, I have to tell you about the coloring. At first I thought she was using a dark makeup but then I see it's her regular

16

color, all over; beige with a little apricot mixed in, really beautiful.

Well, my heart dropped into my shoes. This has got to be Ralphic's girl of course, and it's not enough she should be topless but a little colored besides and when I have to give this information to my sister, I could really end up with a mental case on my hands.

"I'm Vangie Jamison," she says. The voice has got an extra little ring to it, back in the throat. Some actresses have got it, and when they do, they are the exciting ones you don't forget. Like Lynn Fontanne.

"I'm sorry but I don't seem to remember you," the girl says.

Before I can speak Larry says, "You wouldn't, honey. This is our first time at the club. But you were mentioned as one of the main attractions."

"Well, that's nice to hear, but I'm just one of the help. Have you ordered?"

"There's no hurry." I see he's got the charming smile on his face, all ready for action, and just to order a couple of drinks it doesn't pay. "How long have you worked here, Vangie?"

"Not very long," she says, "and I'd better get your order or I may not be here much longer. The management doesn't encourage us to loiter at the tables."

"Yeah, I can see on busy nights it could create a traffic problem." The way he's looking at her and where, it's got a special meaning. "Okay, honey, bring us a couple of J and B's, with short soda." She writes it down. "And maybe something nice to munch on," he says, again looking you know where.

"We've an assortment of canapes," she says. "Would you like a plate of those?"

"Fine," Larry says. "You're a very pretty girl, Vangie. In

fact," he says, looking around, "I'd say you were a stickout."

I'm getting all the time a little smaller in my chair. I make bad jokes myself but this kind of remarks, these girls must hear them five hundred times a night, and even from Shakespeare it would get pretty tiring. But the girl shows nothing in her face except a little smile which you couldn't really call a smile, you could see it's just put on, with the lipstick. What she's thinking, God knows. If it was me, I would be worried for my rating with her as a punster but if Larry worried about things like this he would have been a nervous wreck long ago.

"I'll get your order," she says and walks away, swinging the hips just a little. "That's quite a dish, Morris," Larry says, looking after her. "How long has Ralphie been playing in this league?"

"I don't know. He's a very handsome boy. When he was sixteen my sister had to put in a separate phone for him, for the girls who were calling."

"For herself you mean, so she could listen in." He looks toward the bar now and I see his expression changes a little.

"What is it?" I ask. "You recognize somebody?"

"No. Don't get edgy, Morris. If anybody from your lodge is here, it's not to check on the membership. So he's in the same boat as you are. Why don't you relax and enjoy the scenery."

Well, I didn't think of it before but now I'm starting to get uncomfortable. I don't care what Larry says, I would feel very foolish if anybody I knew saw me in a place like this. I would rather already it would be the whole business and they saw me going into a hotel with a floozie.

"Listen," I said. "I think we better tell the girl — "

"Not so fast," Larry says. "You came out here to find out something about her — "

18

"I don't want to trick her into anything, Larry. Anyway, she seems to be a very nice, refined girl."

He gives me a look full of pity. "You are a wonder, Morris. In the dress business for thirty years — give me a chance to work on this bird a little. And I'll make a tape for you later when the four-letter words start pouring out." He gives another look toward the bar. "I wouldn't be surprised if this could be mob stuff. Little League. I hope young Ralphie hasn't got himself in too deep here. The kid could get hurt."

Well, this is not such a pleasant thought. Seems to me it's a fantasy, from television, but who am I to know about such things? The girl comes back with the drinks and the canapes. Larry throws a ten-dollar bill on the tray.

"We can't stay long, honey," he says. "How about we should meet for a bite of something after you're through here."

"I'm afraid I can't tonight," she says.

He picks up a matchbook from the table, opens it and hands her a pen. "Jot down your phone number, Vangie. I'll give you a ring tomorrow."

"Why don't you give me yours," she says. "I'll call you."

"I'm just in town for a few days this trip. I'd like to get acquainted. I haven't used up my expense account. My boss is a very generous man." Again he turns on the famous Larry smile which I can tell you lots of girls find pretty hard to resist. The girl looks at him a second, then takes the pen and writes in the matchbook.

Larry gives me a look, from the side. Good-bye Ralphie, it says. She closes the matchbook, hands it back to him with the pen.

"I'll call you about noon tomorrow," Larry says. "Okay? Maybe we'll lunch at Lutèce. And take in a matinee after-

19

ward." The matinee he's talking about would draw some crowd on Broadway.

"Sounds lovely," she says. It's a peculiar combination, the smile which is not really a smile and the voice which is sexy, not on purpose, just naturally. Like the color of the skin. "I'd better not dawdle," she says. "The management doesn't like us to make dates on the premises."

"Okay, honey. Take those pretty things away for now. Remember the name. Larry Evans."

She goes away. "Since when are you Larry Evans?" I ask.

"Since I got a look at the management watching us. Over at the bar."

I looked. "How do you know he's watching us."

"I've got a receiver on the back of my neck. It's been beeping for the last five minutes."

"You're imagining things," I said. "He looks like a plain ordinary member of the Mafia to me."

"You're getting to be quite a jokester in your old age, Morris." I wasn't feeling jokey, believe me. "Anyway, I'm taking no chances," Larry says. He opens the matchbook, smiles a little, shows me where the girl wrote her telephone number.

"Well," he says, "mission accomplished."

"You're going to call her?" I said.

"I think so. She turns me on. Reminds me of an English girl I had in the war. Strictly Lady Godiva by day but when the door closed —"

"Larry, I don't need the details. Please. Let's go."

"What's the matter with you," he says. "You sorry for Ralphie now? You want him to marry this?"

I don't know what I wanted. But sorry, I was. I don't know what about exactly. It's a familiar feeling lately. Just sorry. For everything. And everybody.

*

When I got home Sophie was in bed watching an old movie on television. "Hello," she says. She gives me a quick look. "You've got indigestion again. I knew it."

"I haven't got indigestion. I hardly ate anything."

"Did you remember to take the pills?"

"Yes. Is Jenny home?"

"I don't think so. She had a date."

"With whom?"

"Some new man. From Chicago. I think he's an architect."

"What's his name?"

"I forget. Van Leyden. Van Linton. Something with a Van."

"For heaven's sake," I said, kicking off my shoes, "isn't anybody in the family going to settle for a name like Dubinsky or Rosenbaum?"

"Don't get Jenny married every time she goes out with a man. She's twenty-two years old — "

"She's twenty-three years old."

"That's right. March. Morris, stop worrying about her. She wouldn't be an old maid, I promise you."

"This is not what worries me. What is her interest in life, Sophie?" I don't know why, I was thinking about those girls walking around, with the empty look in their eyes. Cigars. Cigarettes.

"Her interest is men," Sophie said, "and clothes. And the theater. And politics. And ceramics. And when it's time for her to get interested in marriage, she'll get married. And if she doesn't it won't be a tragedy either. Marriage is a social convention, not a categorical imperative. People can live without it."

I stared at her. "From where did you get such ideas, Sophie? From Dr. Bernstein's lectures?"

"Morris, we are living in a different world. You want to

fight City Hall, I can't stop you. But not me. I put in my time worrying about the children. Harold has problems with Marie? Let him work them out. Jenny wants to be a free soul? Let her live and be well. I'm not going to make myself miserable. I've got some years left, I'm going to make the most of them. I'm a person too."

"Sophie, have you joined a new club lately? Called, maybe, Women's Liberation?"

"Me? Those *meshugenahs?* Better watch this picture," she said. "Couldn't you faint from that Cary Grant?"

"No," I said. "You want me to faint, I'll look at Ingrid Bergman."

"Both of them. What beautiful people. What is he now, sixty-five? Sixty-seven? This picture was made twelve years ago, so he must have been what — fifty-five. Your age. He looks like a boy there."

"He looks like a boy of fifty-five. And if you ask me, he should have stopped being cute when he was thirty-five."

She gave me another look. "Where did you have dinner?"

"At the Gay Blades Club," I said. "In Weehawken."

"You're making it up," she says.

"Could you stop with the television already. I can't talk against it."

"What is the Gay Blades Club?" she says.

"It's a fencing society," I said. "What else?"

"Morris, stop teasing me. Where were you this evening?"

"I told you. The Gay Blades Club. It's a front for the Mafia. They got topless waitresses there and your nephew Ralphie is mixed up with one of them."

"Bessie's boy?"

"Yes. He wants to marry her."

"Morris," she says. "You want my advice?"

"No. But you're going to give it to me anyway."

"Stay out of it," she says. "Don't interfere."

"It's too late. I did. And I feel real rotten about it. My sister Bessie, God bless her. I wish she would forget my telephone number."

"What happened? Why didn't you tell me about it?"

"Because I knew what you would say. 'Don't interfere.' " I got into bed.

"Please tell me what happened, Morris."

"Some other time," I said. "Go back to your fifty-five-year-old boy, and faint some more. And tomorrow you'll tell me *I'm* the one needs a few sessions with an analyst."

Next afternoon, Larry comes into my office. I see he's got the matchbook in his hand and a very peculiar look on his face.

"You called the number?" I said.

"Yes." He hands me the matchbook. "You call it."

"Why should I call it?"

"Go ahead," he says. "Dial the number."

I did. After the second ring this is what I hear: A recording: "Are you bereft, brother, or sister? Are you a sinner who has lost touch with God? Are you vexed in spirit and sick at heart? It's not too late. Our beloved Saviour holds out his arms to you. This moment, wherever you are, fall on your knees, lift up your eyes and pray with us for grace and forgiveness."

I hung up.

"Those people ought to be stopped," Larry says. "Suppose I was calling from a phone booth. A person could get arrested if he's found kneeling in a phone booth."

I started to laugh, and Larry with me. But I could see he's a little hurt. Somebody like Larry, who's made a career of girls, I guess at his age a little doubt could creep in. Me, I got to tell you I had a sneaky feeling of satisfaction. Who knows, maybe I've been jealous of Larry all these years and I didn't mind at all to see him bump his nose for a change. But the main thing, I had a feeling about this girl last night. Seemed to me, topless or not, there was something fine about her. And I felt good all of a sudden that maybe I wasn't mistaken, after all. I decided I was going out again to the Gay Blades and have a talk with her. Alone.

When I called Sophie to tell her, she says, "Again the Gay Blades? I thought you had it settled last night."

"Well, today it's a different story."

"Morris, you are not going to get into trouble? You haven't been a hero for fifty years. Don't start now."

"What hero?" I said. "I'm going to talk to a very pretty girl and get something straightened out with her."

"You said something about the Mafia last night — "

"I was joking. Forget it."

"Well, I don't approve," she says. "I wish you would not mix into this situation. It's not your business — "

"The family is not my business?" I said. "My sister and my nephew are not my business? To be human and give a damn about somebody is not my business? What is my business, Sophie? To sit and figure out what to put on my tombstone?"

"All right, Morris," she says. "Do what you want. But promise me something. Promise me you wouldn't get into any fights with Ralphie. He is over six feet tall and he's a few years younger than you."

I'm telling you, takes a loving wife to keep a man chopped down to the proper size for home use, every time.

When I came into the Gay Blades Club that evening, I saw the same man at the bar Larry said was watching us. I went up to him. "I would like to talk to Vangie Jamison," I said.

"You were here last night, weren't you," he says. "With a friend."

"Yes," I said. "Last night he did the talking. Tonight I would like a chance."

"Listen," he says, "I sell pipedreams here to old *kockers* at high prices. I don't like to turn away business. But man to man, I see the emblem in your lapel, forget it. You are wasting your time with Vangie."

"I don't want to make a date with her," I said. "I'm Ralph Immerman's uncle — "

"Oh, Ralphie," he says. "*Shalom*. Dave Berman." He puts out his hand and I give him the grip.

"What lodge," he says.

I told him.

"I'm Bensonhurst," he says. "That's a nice boy, your nephew. Of course, I had to throw him out a couple of times. Your name's Immerman? You're not in the business?"

"My name is Seidman, I'm in the dress business. Listen, could you give Vangie an hour off this evening. I would appreciate it, Berman. I got a few things to discuss with her."

"Sure. You want to talk in my office?"

"Thanks. And tell her please to put on something. It's a little embarrassing you know, sitting across from a naked bosom, trying to have a discussion."

"I know what you mean," he says. "To me of course it seems perfectly natural. Only thing that excites me now is to see a girl in a blouse." He laughs. "Listen, I'm not looking a gift horse in the mouth. It's better than when I was selling corned beef sandwiches for ninety cents on Sixth Avenue and getting complaints I didn't put in enough meat. Come on, you'll wait in my office."

25

It takes a while before Vangie comes in. Maybe more time than just to put on the blouse and skirt that make her look now like a schoolgirl. I could see from the look in her eyes that I got trouble.

"Sit down, Vangie," I said. "I want to have a talk with you."

She doesn't sit down. "What about?" she says.

"Mr. Berman told you I'm Ralphie's uncle?"

"Yes. Why didn't you tell me that last night?" I haven't got an answer ready and she says, "You brought that super-annuated charm boy out here to show me up as a tart — "

"I'm sorry, Vangie. It was a very sneaky thing to do, I realize. I got no excuse. I could only ask you to forgive me."

I see the fire dies down in her eyes.

"If you would have seen the charm boy's face after he called the number," I said, "it would have paid you back a little."

A smile comes into her eyes, a little one, but this time it's not just part of the makeup. I couldn't exaggerate to you how relieved I felt. Or how important for me this girl shouldn't think I'm a monster.

"That's a cute trick, Vangie," I said. "You use it often?"

"Not very. It's kind of cruel. I've got another one for the real creeps. The Ninety-fourth Street Precinct Station. I happen to know the sergeant there and he's got something special prepared for anybody who calls up and asks for Vangie."

"Well, you are a girl who knows how to look after herself. I'm glad."

She sits down now. "You wanted to talk to me."

"Yes. We got off to a rotten start. Could we start over and have a frank discussion?"

She gives me a look now, got humor in it but sharp too. "Does that mean I'm supposed to listen while you explain why it's all wrong between Ralph and me?"

26

"It means I will say what I think and you'll say what you think and we'll both try to remember we've got no reason to hate each other. Not me, or you, or Ralphie."

"Why do you call him Ralphie? Makes him sound like a kid on a bicycle. Or maybe that's the idea." And again she gives me that sharp look, like she's going right past my eyes into my head.

"Vangie, don't make everything into a plot. Parents are not conspirators against their children — "

"No? Can I quote you on that? Because there's some other testimony around — "

"You mean Mr. Freud."

"And others. But let's not get bogged down there. We could be a month arguing our way out. You were going to say something."

"I was going to say that maybe, if you listen without a psychiatrist on each elbow, you will hear in the name Ralphie the sound of love, of worry, because he still acts like a kid a lot of the time, not on a bicycle but on a merry-go-round."

"When was the last time you talked to him?"

"You want the truth? Outside the courthouse on Center Street, about a year ago."

"He told me about that. I think you'll find he's changed since then."

"I hope so. But he's still twenty — "

"Twenty-one."

"And you're what — nineteen?"

"Twenty-one. Now you're going to say we're too young to know our own minds."

"I'm not. I'm going to say that youth is wonderful but experience counts for something too."

"Yes. If it's your own. I don't think *your* experience of the world counts for much with those of us who have to live in the world today."

27

"You mean I'm not living in the world today? I got no idea what's going on?"

"I don't mean that at all. But you did say this was to be a frank discussion — "

"Vangie," I said, "did you ever hear of the Talmud?"

"Yes. I've even read some of it. And guess with whom?"

"Ralphie?"

"Yes. And we've read some of the Koran and the Bhagavad Gita and the Kama Sutra — "

"This I figured," I said. "All right. What are these books? Thousands of years of experience."

"Okay. Maybe I was there and I read them now to refresh my memory."

"You're joking, Vangie."

"About reincarnation? No. But just because a thing's old doesn't mean it has to be true. Or good. You dig up a piece of sculpture three thousand years old, if it was done by a good artist, it's good, if it was done by a genius it's a thing of beauty and a joy forever, and if it was done by a hack, it's junk. Some of the Bible or the Koran is true and beautiful, and some of it may have had some relevance at the time but no meaning at all for today, and some of it is just a lot of crap. Now and then. I'll tell you, frankly, Mr. Seidman, that Talmud is a badly overwritten book. Braiding nuances together and coming up with another nuance. That's coffee house stuff. Gets pretty boring."

"Vangie, that book kept the Jews together for two thousand years. Of course, not everybody is so happy about this. If you were an Arab, for instance — "

"I am," she says. "Sort of."

"You're not serious."

"Well, I had a great-grandmother who was a Ranee somewhere in India. Her family were Muslims so she could have

28

been Moorish or Arabian, way back. There's a portrait of her I've seen. In formal dress. Bare to the waist. About my color."

"I see. And you are following in her footsteps."

"Not exactly. I'm missing a rope of emeralds around the neck, big enough to give you curvature of the spine." She gives a laugh now, with that funny extra sound, like there would be chimes in her throat. I'll tell you the truth, for a minute made me feel thirty years younger.

"So that's the complexion," I said.

"You thought I was part Black."

"I thought maybe. Anyway, gives you a marvelous coloring. You are a lucky girl — you got your own Miami Beach built in."

"But if it were Hamitic blood instead of Aryan Indian, that would have bothered you, wouldn't it? Maybe it does anyway."

"Me, no. I would feel like an idiot to have such a prejudice. Don't forget, I'm only an honorary member of the Establishment. Ralph elected me. There's still plenty places where I'm only a sheeny. Or a kike. So I should look down my nose at anybody? But remember, I'm Ralphie's uncle, not his mother."

"I think he'd be better off if you were both." She gives me the quick smile. "Mr. Seidman, let me get you straight about Ralph and me. We've got a lot going for us in our relationship. We feel alike about most things. We turn each other on and we don't need gin or pot to hit E above high C in bed."

She gives me suddenly a look like she realized she's talking to a man, a stranger, and not to a girl friend. "Have I embarrassed you?"

"Well, this is supposed to be a frank discussion between

29

us," I said, "so I could tell you, frankly, in my day young girls weren't so frank. But I'm not embarrassed. You are a decent girl and you are telling me honestly about your feelings. Actually, I'm flattered you're not talking to me like I would be somebody left over from the Stone Age. I've got a daughter, she's approximately your age, it's a couple of years now that she stopped talking to me altogether. I don't mean she's sore at me or anything, she's just got nothing to say to me, and vice versa. No communication. I'll bet you heard that word before. No meaningful dialogue. No more advice from papa. Just pony up the allowance and don't bother me. Well, this is another subject. Honest feelings — what's to be embarrassed about? Or shocked. It's only the rotten things in the world that really shock me, Vangie, the cruel things. What people do to each other — this shocks me. Still. After a lifetime. I should be used by now."

"You're very nice," she says. "And I've got good news for you to carry to Ralph's mother. I've no intention of marrying him."

"Does he know this?"

"He should. We've talked about it enough."

"You want to tell me why?"

"I've got other plans for my life, that's all. For one thing I want to finish school — "

"You're going to school?"

"Yes. Barnard. I've lost some time, moving around, but I'm finishing up this year."

"You're studying for something? I mean something special?"

"Yes, archaeology. That's my major."

"You want to be an archaeologist?"

"Uh huh. I've got the place picked out where I'd like to work. Mexico. Yucatán, probably."

"Yucatán. This is where the Aztecs came from?"

"No. The Mayans."

"Oh yes. They are the ones made the funny calendar, with twenty days — "

"No, those were the Aztecs." She gave me another smile, for real, not the customer smile. "I've got a fascinating book on the Mayans I'll let you have, if you're interested."

"I'm always interested to learn something, Vangie. When this stops I'll know it's time for me to check in with the *malchamovess.*"

"What's that?"

"That's someone looks like Bela Lugosi, with the black cape."

"A vampire?" She looked puzzled.

"The boss vampire, Vangie. He's the angel of death. He's been flying around our apartment lately, to remind me we've got a date one of these days."

"Oh, come on, Mr. Seidman. That must have been Batman you saw."

I laughed and she joined in, then I said, "What about Ralph? He doesn't fit into the plan for your future? Not even to handle a shovel?"

The smile went away from her face. "Hold on now," I said. "We're getting to be friends, don't cross me off because I made a bad joke. It's a weakness of mine."

"I'll tell you something, Mr. Seidman. Might interest you and Ralph's mother. My parents would have a fit if I told them I was going to marry a Jew."

"But that you walk around half naked in this club every night, this doesn't bother them."

"I think it bothers them. But there's always that picture of great-grandmama. And I send them fifty dollars a week. That carries a little weight too."

"I guess the Ranee's emeralds didn't come down to your family."

"No. That was a bummer. I understand there were trunks full of the stuff. She ran off with an Englishman of high degree, as Baroness Orczy would put it, but not high enough to keep her from being tossed out of the family. He tried growing rubber, and then exporting copra or something, and then smuggling I suspect; the record's sketchy there and I'd guess he ended up in the clink or in a Singapore alley with a knife in his back. I always used to think of him in the uniform of a Bengal Lancer, like Gary Cooper, riding off on a dangerous mission from which he never returned. Anyway, my father's descended from that line. He's in the insurance business in Montreal. Not very good at it, as you must have guessed. He prefers to shoot. My mother's half French. Which makes me one-quarter Canuck, I guess. And three-quarters confused."

"Well, you've got quite a history. Tell me, it doesn't bother you, this — "

"You mean this sleazy business. No. It's very simple, Mr. Seidman. It's a night-time job and leaves me my days free for school. I get a chance to do some of my reading during breaks here and on the bus back and forth. I make between a hundred and fifty and two hundred dollars a week and that's a lot better than I can do selling girdles at one of the department stores or being a secretary."

"A good secretary makes good money."

"Anybody who paid me that kind of money to be a secretary, with my experience, or lack of it, would expect fringe benefits that would go way beyond just having a look. I'm not too fond of being gaped at, frankly, but I've rationalized it. It's a job, I'm using my assets, so to speak, I've learned how to handle the customers and I don't lose any sleep over

32

the propriety of what I'm doing. Ralph and I argue about it every once in a while but I can always get him on the freedom of action clause in our contract."

She stopped for a minute and looked past me. "Ralph's a beautiful boy," she said.

Well, this kind of rocks me, you know. I never thought of Ralphie as a beautiful boy, just as a nuisance.

"I have my problems with him, of course," she said. "He wanted to hang around here every night and we had a few stormy sessions before I put a stop to that. Then there's sex," she says. "Tell me, Mr. Seidman, do Jewish boys have an idea that if they're not balling — I mean having sex all the time, they'll get sick or something?"

I tried to look like this would be a normal question for me, the kind I hear every day. "Well, I'm not really an authority," I said. "But I'll ask our rabbi, and I'll have an answer for you next week."

She gives again that laugh, could make a person jealous of his own nephew. "We almost broke up a few months ago; it was about college. I don't care about marks really, it's what you come away with that counts, but I think a C average for anyone as bright as Ralph is, is a disgrace. Besides you can't last with that kind of grade; sooner or later he'd have to be dropped or drafted. So I told him he'd better forget about the placards and demonstrations and the heavy sex for a while and start getting some work done. Well, he got livid, told me I was a political moron, with no sense of the real values and I said if being a political genius meant getting bounced from school to school with mama and papa or uncle footing the bill, I didn't go for it and we could stop seeing each other right then."

She gives me a funny look now, like a little girl showing a new dress. "You wouldn't know about Ralph's marks this last term, I guess. An A, two A minuses and two B's. That's a little different than it's been."

I should say a little different. Well, this is some wonderful girl I met by accident and what I'm thinking about now is how I could get her into the family, not keeping her out.

"Listen," I said, "I think it's very sensible that you don't want to tie yourself down to marriage yet. But you are not the kind of girl who is going to play around, making experiments — "

"I can't know that yet," she says. "Maybe I will."

"I'll guarantee you. I'm a pretty good judge of human nature and it didn't change so much in the last thirty, forty years. I could see this is not just a passing thing between you and Ralphie — "

"How can you tell?"

"I wish I could say back to you, just the way you said it to me, 'Ralph is a beautiful boy.' " Something happened in her eyes. Something very nice. Should happen to a girl's eyes who's interested in you. "And sooner or later," I said, "it wouldn't be enough for you, weekends and so on. I don't care how modern you think you are, you will want a home, and a family, and a settled life — "

"I doubt it. Anyway, it's not anything I want to think about now."

"But think about this. This is no job for a high class girl like you. Don't tell me it's the same as your great-grandmother, she walked around also with a bare bosom. It was the style of the country, a whole different thing, she was dressed up, or down, to meet high class people. Doesn't it bother you that you are spending a big piece of your life with those faces out there?"

"I thought I explained that. It's two hundred dollars a week, more or less. And I don't know where else I can earn that kind of money."

34

"I'm coming to that. I got something to suggest. I would like you to be a model in our place. You'll figure out your average earnings here for the last few months and this will be your salary. How about it?"

She doesn't say anything for a minute. Her eyes got a kind of smoky look now and I can't tell what she is thinking. There is something a little foreign about her, maybe oriental, I don't know. "Well, it's rather an attractive idea," she says finally. "But I don't know. Is that the kind of salary models usually make? I don't want to become one of your philanthropies, Mr. Seidman."

"Don't be ridiculous. I'm semi-retired but I'm still a businessman. For a good model two hundred a week is not unusual in our line. We'll get our money's worth out of you, don't worry."

"I always thought I was too big here to be a dress model."

"Ordinarily this would be true. But I've got an idea in mind. We'll start designing dresses for girls instead of boys. Will be a big revolution in the dress business. Couple of Paris designers will kill themselves, which will be a pleasure. You will become famous; Vangie Jamison, the girl who took the bust out of *Playboy* and put it back in the fashion magazines. We'll make a fortune. We'll have to raise your salary. And the family will be satisfied — I know right now this is not a consideration," I said, quick, "but it can't hurt. You know I've got a daughter-in-law who was a model."

"Really?"

"When my Harold married her, it was a crisis in the family. My sister Bessie had to write to Dear Abby to make sure it was okay for her to come to the wedding. Now modeling is a regular, respectable profession with her. Do it, Vangie. Would make things a lot simpler for all of us."

"I don't know," she says. "I'd have to rearrange my whole schedule — "

35

"You'll excuse me if I'm getting too personal but I think this would be a good thing too. It's too much, what you are doing, working at night and school in the day and homework in-between. And Ralph. It's all right now, at your age you could get away with it for a while. But would be better to have a more sensible routine. We could work out something about the hours in the shop, the mornings are usually not busy with us, and you could maybe cut down on the courses at college. So you'll be an archaeologist a year later. But a healthy one."

I had in mind, to tell you the truth, maybe she wouldn't be an archaeologist at all but a lawyer's wife, with a house in Long Island and a garden she could dig in when she got the urge.

"I'll think about it," she said.

"Talk to Ralphie about it too," I said. "Him it wouldn't hurt to have an incentive to work a little harder, finish up his school so he could start to make a living, for both of you."

"What happens if we decide in a year or so that we don't belong together anymore?"

"What happens, Vangie, if somebody drops the first bomb and then there will be only two Chinese and one Russian from Uzbek left to be archaeologists? One thing at a time, yes?"

She gives me a smile and says, "I'm going to have a talk with Ralph about something else. He said you were square."

"He's not the only one. You should talk to my daughter. Where do you live, Vangie?"

"West Eighty-eighth Street."

"Manhattan? They supply you transportation from here?"

"No. There's no problem. I take a bus to a hundred and twenty-fifth and the subway from there, or a taxi if I'm feeling rich."

36

"That's not such a good thing, a girl alone, two, three o'clock in the morning."

"I can take care of myself," she says. "You said so yourself."

"Yes, but in that jungle, at night? I know on television it looks easy. All the girls are karate experts."

This time she gives me a full smile. She's a wonderful-looking girl, high cheekbones, full mouth and very white teeth. "I know a few tricks," she said. "I played hockey in school. And I've got a very piercing scream. And the taxi drivers are all my friends."

"I don't like it," I said. "I'm going to talk to Ralphie about it. You should have a car."

"I wish you wouldn't," she says. "Ralph wouldn't appreciate it. And neither do I. I like to feel I can manage my own life. Without interference — however well meaning. Now *I've* been very frank. I hope you don't mind."

Was wonderful. Polite, neat, T.O.T. "*Está entendido,* as we say in Spanish," I said. "And not from Berlitz, I want you to understand. I got it, authentic, from a waitress in Madrid."

"You've been to Spain?"

"Yes. Spent more than a month there. I could recommend it for your honeymoon."

She laughs. "I'll keep it in mind. You're a very charming man, Mr. Seidman."

"Thank you. You could have me in your family if you want." She gives me a look and then we both laugh. "All right, I'll stop being a *shatchen.* You know what this is?"

"A marriage broker?"

"Yes."

She says the word now. "Your accent is very good," I said. "Would be a cinch to get you into Hadassah." I was feel-

37

ing pretty good, I tell you. Like I would have had a couple drinks. "I'm hungry, you know," I said. "Would you like to eat something with me?"

"I'd love to. But I don't think Mr. Berman — "

"Mr. Berman is a brother Mason. He doesn't know it yet but he's giving you this evening off. You are my guest."

Driving across the bridge with her, I remembered something from long ago, when I was courting Sophie, she lived in New Jersey those days and I still lived at home with my mother on Delancey Street. There was still the Weehawken ferry then, it ran until midnight and I could catch the last boat because in those days you didn't keep a girl out until three, four in the morning. I would stand in front by the rail and look down at the water and you know how it really is, the Hudson there, dirty, full of junk, garbage. It was the same in those days too, but in the dark, mixed up with the lights and your own thoughts, you saw only the mystery, the river going into the sea, joining up all the lovers in the world, all places and all times. I was a member of a big lodge, with a secret password and the secret was you should never say aloud what you were feeling. Because then it would be just words. Unless you were a poet. Then you were allowed. To try, at least. But if not, you kept your feelings to yourself. And as long as you kept your mouth shut, then you were no more a greenhorn (that was the word those days, not very friendly, believe me) not just a cutter in a skirt factory living in a flat on the East Side, over a poultry store. You were one of a goodly company, like Shakespeare says, you put your hand out there in the dark and gave the grip to all your lodge brothers, to that Greek boy who swam the Hellespont, and all the others, you were part of the same story, maybe the oldest and best in the world.

38

Yes, my writer friend, I guess the most wonderful thing to be is a lover when you are young. And maybe the next best, a poet when you are old.

"Your face is a study, Mr. Seidman," I heard the girl say. I looked at her, she was smiling, she looked beautiful and pure, like every girl who is twenty-one should look. "I was thinking about things," I said.

"Shoes and ships and sealing wax?"

"Love, if you want to know. Vangie, you talk very modern about your feelings for Ralphie. How you like the same things, how you could hit E above high C in bed — you know what is the worst thing we did to you, our generation? Why you should really hate us? I don't know how, but we took away the mystery from your lives. You don't know what it is to worship anymore, to be in love, you feel foolish even when you say the word. Isn't this true?"

I saw she was shaking her head. "No. It's true that I don't use the word because it doesn't have any meaning for me. There's a lot of romantic bull — of cant — mixed up in it. And I want the words I use to mean what I mean. If I don't know what I mean, it's better to shut up. But that doesn't signify I'm incapable of any deep feeling. Just the opposite. I'm trying — and I'm not the only one, I've got lots of company — to cut through the layers of crap to the real gutty thing that's only diminished by words. If Ralph said to me 'parting is such sweet sorrow' or 'a music in my feet has led me to your chamber window, sweet' I'd drop a vase on his head. But when he's asleep in my arms, with that mop of blue black hair rumpled around his face, I think I know what mystery is, and reverence for what people feel for each other, when they're not hating, or promoting or bullshitting. I'm sorry. That just slipped out."

"It's all right, I heard the word before. Vangie, I don't

39

think you realize, you are paying me the biggest compliment when you talk to me straight, like to one of your friends. You don't know what a privilege this is. Please continue."

"Well, I don't think the basic feelings change. I think they can be dimmed by sham and hypocrisy and if I understand what's going on, that's the big gripe the kids have against the hydra head of parent-teacher-boss-congressman. Endless, self-righteous bullshit. But real feelings don't change. They're there, the way they've always been. Along the Nile, or the Tiber, or the Hudson." She looked up out of the car window, at the sky. "I wouldn't be surprised if even those little green people up there on Mars, with the pointy heads, belonged to the club."

It was like magic, you know, like our thoughts would have crossed each other, there on the bridge, in the dark.

Well, you can imagine, I couldn't wait to talk to my sister Bessie next day. I got her on the phone and I said, "All right, Bessie. I had a talk with the girl. There wouldn't be any marriage."

"Thank God!" she says. And then, "What did she say?"

"She said she's got no plans to marry Ralphie. It's not even in her mind right now."

"Is that so? What other plans has she got? Miss de Milo from Weehawken?"

"What do you care, Bessie? You were worried Ralphie is going to marry her. So you can stop worrying. There wouldn't be a wedding."

"She's got somebody better than Ralphie?"

"I didn't ask her. But could be. She is some beautiful girl, Bessie."

"So this is what I worked myself up to? Even for a girl in a joint, my son isn't good enough?"

"She likes him," I said. "They get along well. He amuses her. For the time being."

"Amuses her! A fire on her."

"But for marriage, no."

"What's wrong with him? A boy six foot two, looks like a movie actor — "

"Bessie, you want me to go back now and see if maybe I could talk her into marrying him?"

"Don't be so smart. I just want to know how she's got the nerve, a girl like this. When will she get another opportunity, a boy like Ralphie."

"When?" I say. "Every five minutes. You should have a look at this girl. She's a dream."

"Sure. A dream. Walking around with a naked chest in everybody's face."

"She goes to Barnard," I said. "She is a straight A student." This I didn't know but I figured I'm entitled to a little bonus for my trouble.

"What are you telling me?" she says.

"I'm telling you this girl is putting herself through college, she sends money home to her parents besides, she is beautiful, brilliant, and she doesn't want to marry your Ralphie."

"Is she Jewish?" she says.

"She is not Jewish. Her family is from India. Her great-grandmother was a cousin of the lady who is buried in the Taj Mahal."

"So this is the reason," Bessie says. "I figured, a girl like this, what could she be but an anti-Semite."

"What do you care what she is?" I said. "Your brother came through for you. He did the job. You could relax, go back to your television. Ralphie is not going to get married to a topless girl in New Jersey."

41

"You know, Morris," she says, "sometimes I wonder if it wouldn't be a good thing for this boy to settle down already, stop bumming around."

"Who would support him?"

"We could help out. And you could help out. Take it off your income tax."

"Since when is a nephew who wants to get married a deduction?"

"Never mind. You could afford it. Plenty of families are doing this now with the children who are in school."

"Well, you got to find him a girl first," I said. "Ask around among your friends in Flushing. Maybe some nice girl will turn up."

I'm really rubbing it in now. I guess I've got a cruel streak. "Oh, one other thing, Bessie," I say. "She is coming to work for me, as a model. I wanted to tell you, in case you are coming to the shop, let me know first so I'll arrange you shouldn't have to meet her."

And I hang up. I haven't had such a good time since I don't know when.

Well, the next thing of course, I get a visit from Ralphie. I'm not sure what to expect with this boy. The last time I saw him I had to go down to court and sign an affidavit that I would pay for a plate glass window in a certain coffee house where he threw a chair at someone's head and broke the window instead.

"I guess I'm supposed to thank you," he said to me that time outside the courthouse.

"Don't be hasty," I told him. "Think it over a few days. Don't forget, it's dirty money I squeezed out of my workers."

"You think I'm kind of an idiot, don't you, Uncle Morris?"

"Did I ever say so?"

"No. Not out loud."

"Then what are you putting words in my mouth? Listen," I said, "your mother asked me, I came down here, I settled the thing with the restaurant man. I don't want your thanks, good-bye, give my regards home in case you are planning to pay a visit there sometime and do me a favor, next time try to find a soft chair."

"Don't you want to know what it was all about?" he says.

"What's the difference?" I said. "You struck a blow for justice against the Establishment, of this I'm sure."

"I struck a blow against a black bastard who was a mile high on speed and singing a ditty about getting the Jew Communists off the black man's back. The next verse is about the Jew landlords and the Jew bankers. The verse that's missing is the one about the idiot Jews who give fund-raising parties for these sons of bitches."

"So you threw a chair, and broke a window, and now the whole problem is solved. If you broke his head instead of the window, would have been an even better solution."

"Look, Uncle Morris, that's all very reasonable but not everybody can just sit by and watch these curiosities happen, from the club window. We're not that calm and collected."

"Listen, Ralphie," I said. "I had enough with you this afternoon, I don't need now an argument about me and my club members and how we failed our responsibility to turn the world into a paradise for you, with two motorcycles in every garage and marijuana growing in the back yard. I'm going back to my shop and would be a good idea if you would get back to school and start to learn something about the law. Because with your temper, the way you are going, you will need a full-time lawyer, just for yourself."

Reminded me a little bit about the arguments I used to have with Harold when he came home from the army. He

43

was mad at the whole world. Particularly me, because somehow I was responsible for those people he saw in Korea, long after the war still following the garbage trucks to pick up the scraps that fell off. I suppose nowadays the youngsters got good reason to be angry and confused too, with the business in Viet Nam. Anyway, this what I just told you was the last time I had seen Ralphie, it was about a year before. One afternoon, a few days after I had the talk with Vangie, the reception girl calls me in my office to say my nephew is out front.

"Frisk him," I said. "And send him in."

"I beg your pardon, Mr. Seidman?"

"Don't mind me, Miss Weintraub. I'm feeling a little euphoric today. If you don't know what this is, it's a psychological expression for something, could be good or could be bad. If you are a manic depressive, it's bad. If you are semi-retired and getting senile from sitting behind a smoky walnut desk with nothing to do, it's very good. Send in my nephew."

Well, even with the report I got from Vangie, I was surprised at the change. First thing, before he comes into my office, he knocks. You think maybe this is a small thing. For a boy like Ralphie it's a revolution. Then I see he shaved off the beard, he's wearing a regular suit, with a tie. And, most of all, he hasn't got that wild look in his eye. I'm getting a little worried the draft board shouldn't send for him for another examination. Like this, looks like he would pass. Quick.

"What can I do for you, Ralphie," I say. Too easy, I'm not going to make it for him.

"Vangie told me you were out to see her the other night."

"That's right. And I warn you, if you start throwing chairs, this time you'll go to jail."

Right away I felt sorry. "Look, Uncle Morris," he says,

44

"give me a chance. I always get off on the wrong foot with you — "

"All right, Ralphie. Sit down. You want a cup of coffee or something?"

"No thanks. You made quite a hit with Vangie."

"She made quite a hit with me too. If you wouldn't fly off the handle I'll tell you something. I figure if this girl found something in you to love, must be something about you I didn't give you credit for all these years."

He sits, looking down at his hands and I thought, how much they take out of us, how they squeeze us dry, our kids, how much understanding and patience they think they got coming from us, how little they give us back if you want to measure it with a ruler, or weigh it on a scale, and still we've got to give it, regardless; whenever we hold back, the full measure, we feel like monsters sooner or later.

"She told me about the offer you made her," Ralphie says. "I think it was very generous."

"Wasn't generous. It was a business proposition. She'll earn her salary."

"Well, I'm all for it but she's decided no. She says it'll louse things up for her at college. I guess it's something more, actually. I don't think she wants to get too involved with the family."

"I understand. I'm sorry. This is a wonderful girl and I don't like that atmosphere for her at the Gay Blades, whatever happens between you two. She's a very level-headed girl, but she's only twenty-one after all."

"I know, Uncle Morris. I wish I could pry her loose but I don't really feel I've got a right to throw my weight around, telling her what to do. Not in the position I'm in." He stops for a minute. "And I've got another problem. Ma wants to meet her."

45

"You're not serious."

"I almost fell over," he says. "She says she wants to meet this Mohammedan princess I'm not good enough for. Where'd she get the idea Vangie's Mohammedan?"

"From me, I guess. I always forget, I shouldn't make jokes with your mother."

"Well, what am I going to do? I'm scared pissless — excuse me — I'm scared stiff of what'll happen if those two get together. You've got to help me out, Uncle Morris."

So where am I? Mr. Fixit? In the middle, of course, between Vangie and my sister in Longchamps for lunch, a couple of days later. Bessie is wearing her hat with the feathers so I know I could expect the worst. And she doesn't disappoint me. In one minute flat we are in trouble.

"Would you like a drink to start?" I ask Vangie.

"She doesn't need a drink to start," Bessie says. "A girl her age. In the middle of the day."

"I'd like a martini, please," Vangie says. I call over the waiter and tell him to bring a martini and a Scotch. "Plymouth gin if you've got it," Vangie says. They've got it, the waiter tells her. She gives him a big smile, like they stocked it specially for her.

My sister is watching her like she would be performing on a trapeze. "They gave you a good training in that joint in New Jersey," she says. "You order a drink like a real professional."

"Thank you," Vangie says, very quiet. "Why don't you have something too, Mrs. Immerman."

"I should poison my system with that stuff? I drink wine once a year, that's enough for me. Sacramental wine. At Passover. I don't suppose you know what this is."

"I've attended a Passover service," Vangie says, still in the same low voice. I wish she would raise it a little because it's making me nervous. I got a feeling in a couple of minutes

46

dishes could be flying around. "At the home of one of my Jewish friends in high school," she says.

"You understood what was going on?"

"I read the libretto beforehand. In English. The plot seems a little contrived and it could stand some cutting, but I enjoyed it."

"That's nice," Bessie says. "I'm glad you enjoyed it. Couldn't compare, of course, with your Mohammedan holidays."

"Let's order," I said. "We could continue the conversation later."

But doesn't help. Bessie is red in the face and Vangie has got fireworks in her eyes. "I got a couple questions I want to ask you, young lady," Bessie says.

I'm watching those Roman candles in Vangie's eyes, waiting to see when they will go off. Fortunately, the waiter comes now with her drink, he puts it down in front of her and she picks up the glass and swallows half. Then she says, "What would you like to know, Mrs. Immerman?"

"First of all one question. If you think you got something to be stuck up about your family I could tell you that we are Caens, Ralphie's family were priests in Jerusalem, the highest class; for two thousand years we had important people in every country in the world, except maybe India, because nobody ever heard of it, in the governments and the universities, professors, doctors, philosophers, writers, lawyers by the dozen — "

"And don't forget we invented diabetes," I said. "Bessie, you said you were going to ask a question and instead you make an oration. Save it for the United Jewish Appeal. What is the question?"

So she says to Vangie, "The question is why is my Ralphie not good enough for you?"

"For heaven's sake, Bessie," I say, "this is an idea you got

47

stuck in your head, I don't know from where. Miss Jamison doesn't have to advertise for boy friends, she picked out Ralphie, she is very fond of him, she thinks he is a fine boy — "

"But not to get married."

"That's got nothing to do with Ralph," Vangie says. "I just don't want to be married. To anyone."

"So why are you wasting my boy's time?"

Vangie swallows the rest of her drink. Me, I don't know whether I should laugh or send for the police. "Can we change the subject, Mrs. Immerman?" Vangie says. "I've been admiring your hat. Is it a Mr. John?"

"It's a Sarah Fineberg from Flushing. Your mother gets her hats from Mr. John?"

"My mother wears bandanas," Vangie says, "and reads tea leaves. And in between she's generally sozzled. Could I have another martini, Mr. Seidman?"

I called over the waiter.

"What is going on here?" Bessie says.

"If you'll be quiet a minute," I said, "I will order another martini for Miss Jamison. Plymouth gin, like last time," I said to the waiter, "and hold the fruit." The girl gives me her wonderful smile, like a private Hanukkah present. By now I'm sure Bessie is convinced we're in a plot against her, she's so aggravated even the feathers on her hat are standing up.

"You ask me for lunch," she says, "for this purpose? She should sit and get drunk and insult me with cracks about my hat?"

Well, I had enough. "Listen to me, Bessie," I said, "this girl has got the patience of a saint or she would have pulled that hat off your head altogether. Now I've had enough from you. If I hear one more word, I'll get up and walk out with

48

Miss Jamison, and leave you to drive the management crazy."

So now Bessie takes out a handkerchief and starts to cry. "Everybody is against me," she says. "To my son I'm a monster, to my husband I'm an interference for his pinochle, to my brother I'm an ignoramus, a nothing. I come here to have a nice talk with a girl who is going to be my daughter-in-law and right away she is against me too."

I get a look from Vangie now like she would be saying, "Okay, I'll do my best but don't blame me if this ends up in the lobby of the Good Samaritan hospital."

"I'm not against you, Mrs. Immerman," she says. "Why don't you relax? I'm not going to be your daughter-in-law. I'm not going to be anybody's daughter-in-law — "

"What is it, you're a member of some Free Love Society, or what?" Bessie says. A genius, this woman. In her specialty she's got absolutely no competition. Luckily the waiter comes up now with Vangie's drink and she swallows again half, like before, and then she says, "Let's talk about Ralph, Mrs. Immerman. You know, he thinks the world of you. Was he always so handsome?"

This girl, I'm telling you, not to fall in love with her in two minutes you would have to be from wood.

"Handsome," Bessie says. "You think now he is handsome? You should have seen when he was a baby. I couldn't wheel him half a block in his carriage, people would start following, it would be like Easter Sunday on Fifth Avenue."

"What happened to Purim on Delancey Street?" I said. She pays no attention. "He had a head full of curls, I'm telling you, like a Borachello angel."

"You discovered a new Renaissance painter?" I said. "Who's Borachello?"

You understand, I'm not helping the situation with this kind of questions but with a certain kind of pretense I react like I would be stuck with a pin. I can't help myself. I'm in dutch with plenty of people because of it. Well, Bessie is going on now about Ralphie, his curls, the head that's under the curls, if only he would use it to make something of himself instead of trying to knock down the whole system with it. If only the right girl would take him in hand he could be anybody, a Disraeli, a Felix Frankfurter, a Brandeis —

"I'll hold still for some baby pictures," Vangie says, "if you have any."

My sister Bessie carries always a purse that's big as a suitcase and just happens now it's full of pictures of Ralphie, from when he was six months old with his behind to the camera. I kept myself back from asking where is the one where he's got on a suit with stripes and a number, and the afternoon went by now, not a disaster after all. What a girl.

Oh, I've got to tell you something funny. There's a rabbi came a couple of years ago to my sister's congregation in Flushing, and if you are getting in your mind a picture of somebody with a beard and a skull cap, forget it, the new crop of rabbis coming up these years all look like they graduated from Princeton. Well, suddenly, my sister is getting active in the affairs of the temple and besides finding out that the rabbi is very partial to potato pancakes, she is also becoming an authority on Judaic history. She knows, for instance, that the Old Testament is part of the Mohammedan bible too, both religions started out in the same part of the world and many ways they are similar. Jehovah and Allah could be from the same *yeshivah,* Moses is a big man with the Mohammedans also and Jesus is okay with them too, so long as he doesn't mix in about those four *houris* who are

50

waiting in paradise for every Moslem that lives a good kosher life.

I tried to explain to Bessie that if she is becoming an authority on comparative religion to impress Vangie she is giving herself headaches for nothing because Vangie is not a Mohammedan, maybe her great-grandmother was but she married an Englishman and now the family are Episcopalians.

"That's supposed to be an improvement?" Bessie says. To keep up with this woman's logic you've got to be a mental kangaroo. "I don't know if it's an improvement," I said. "It just happened that way."

"So it'll happen in this generation there'll be another change," she says and she's got the rabbi now on a secret mission, he should be around, eating potato pancakes, whenever Vangie comes to visit.

Well, you would think that this whole thing is like *kinderspiel* but funnily enough Vangie tells me the other day that she is getting very interested in Judaism, it's really a system of ethics and aside from the rituals and the dietary laws and so on, it's got less nonsense to it than other religions. You understand, nonsense is my word not hers. She's got a different one she uses to express the same idea, I have to confess I'm never comfortable with it, it always sounds to me like it should be coming from the mouth of someone who is leaning out, drunk, with the hair wild, from a tenement window, not a girl like this who looks like she would be at home at a dinner party in the White House, and with a mind to match any professor's. You can imagine how I felt the first time I heard my own daughter, Jenny, use it. All I could think of was I'm glad my mother is not alive to hear this, she would think the world is coming to an end. And who knows, maybe it is and these are the symptoms.

51

You see how I fell into a trap just now? Those little cap- illaries in the brain. You've got to watch out every min- ute, you shouldn't get fixed in your ideas when you're get- ting old. I said, maybe the world is coming to an end. I should have said *my* world. Theirs is only beginning and I wish I could tell you I would like to be around to see it. Frankly, I'm glad I wouldn't be. This is not a good way to feel, I'm not proud of it. Puts me in a class with the people, a few hundred years ago, who must have thought that if you stopped burning witches the world would go to the dogs.

All my life I've been curious, what will the world be like when there's no more cancer or hunger, when we've discov- ered maybe there are some kind of creatures living on Mars or Venus, when machines will do most of the work and peo- ple will have time to think, to loaf a little and invite their souls, like Whitman says. I wonder what he would say if he could see the kids on the Spanish Steps in Rome, inviting their souls, passing around the marijuana cigarettes and peeing on the balustrades. Next door is the house where Keats lived. "Beauty is truth, truth beauty, that is all ye know on earth and all ye need to know." I don't like what's happening, my friend, I don't understand it, and it's not easy for me to keep saying to myself, an intelligent person has got to keep an open mind.

Anyway, I'm getting accustomed to hear Vangie say non- sense in her language, and doesn't seem strange anymore that in the next breath she could be reciting from the Song of Songs, or rattling off the names of Aztec or Mayan gods I couldn't pronounce them in a hundred years — and then that girl, what was the picture, they had in it a Jewish wed- ding, my sister Bessie wanted to start a boycott in Flushing and she wrote to the producer he should only choke to death in a tub of halvah — yes, *Goodbye, Columbus.* I enjoyed it

52

but that was some portrait of Jews, the scenario could have been written by Goebbels. I haven't figured out about this man Roth, he's a very talented fellow but it's a complicated story there, I think. One of the big mysteries to me is a person who's got problems, from inside, about being a Jew. From outside, is another story. But seems to me if you got some pride, if you are not made of some kind of soup, you get only more stubborn about holding up your head and saying you are a Jew, and if anybody doesn't like it, they could lump it. Maybe, actually, it depends on the parents. I had a Jewish mother, and seems to me I couldn't have been luckier. I would put her up against any heroine I ever heard about, or read about.

But I was saying, the girl in the picture was nice, up until the end. I was surprised to see her name is McGraw, so Irish. I thought actually she was a good-looking Jewish girl from New Jersey or Westchester, I've seen dozens like her, my own Jenny could be her cousin. And then, in *Love Story*, she was also nice and the way she used this word to answer practically every question, even with children, by the time the movie was over I got kind of used to the idea that this is part of the vocabulary of young people now and you got to accept it. Myself, I would be uncomfortable to say it, not because it's dirty but it still sounds to me somehow ugly. Like other words I read now, they're synonyms for girl, or love — tell me, it's such a rich language, English, there's so many ways to describe things, I'm flabbergasted sometimes when I look in Roget's Thesaurus. For an author it must be like the witch's house in Hansel and Gretel, which goody to pick — and from all this riches when you've got to use words like cunt and fuck and bullshit, isn't this kind of a bankruptcy, some way?

Well, the main thing, I'm getting some idea from Vangie

53

how young people think nowadays. It's not right just to be impatient and criticize. I want to understand. Try, at least. After all, it would help me to have some clues with Jenny. What I noticed with the kids, you can't talk to them. They close up. It's like in their minds they got the idea, what is the use to talk to a Hottentot about relevance? Sometimes I get a feeling that they are not really interested in an education anymore, except it's a specialty, like doctor, or lawyer, or how to make Dow Chemical Company miserable. This is for me especially hard to understand. I wanted to swallow everything, whole shelves in the library, it made me actually unhappy to realize I would never be able to read everything that was written in my lifetime, could be this is a kind of megalomania too, on a different level from the dictators. But it's a real puzzle to me how youngsters with all the opportunity could turn their backs to the past. It's like in the Bible Esau sold his birthright for a mess of pottage, instead of pot, only he was tricked, cheated, and now the young people are doing it themselves, on purpose. It's not relevant, they say, and throw away everything that could give them an inkling who they are, what they are.

But not Vangie. Would surprise you how much this girl knows, already, at twenty-one. History, philosophy, religion — I could bet you she holds her own with that rabbi on Judaism. I would like to see his face when she tells him that a lot of the Talmud is coffee house stuff and the *bruchas* are only another kind of voodoo against the Evil Eye. A girl like this makes you realize you shouldn't say young people are this way or that way. There's still differences. Wouldn't surprise me, if you could even find somewhere a girl who dreams about falling in love and getting married. What Vangie dreams about is to be an archaeologist. This is her passion. If someone would put her in a dig in Yucatán, with a

54

shovel and a whisk broom, and occasionally send her in a martini and a sandwich, she would have a happy life. So she says. Maybe she's exaggerating but, you know, I love her for this. To have a passion for something, so long it's not golf, or killing Jews, is to me, the most wonderful thing in life. I'm sorry for the kids who will never know what it is.

I started lately to read some archaeology books and I could understand the fascination. It's like detective stories, how just from digging up pieces of pots and bones and tablets with inscriptions that have been buried hundreds, thousands of years, these scholars could put together whole civilizations, pieces of history that got wiped out by volcanoes or a change of climate, or invasions, or something.

The Gay Blades Club? No, she's not working there anymore. I called up the owner, Dave Berman, I told you he's a brother Mason, and I explained him that Vangie is studying to become a Jew, like Elizabeth Taylor, and she'll maybe one day be a member of my family and he could see right away it doesn't fit for a nice Jewish girl to be a topless waitress. I told him there was a little problem because she's got a mind of her own and she doesn't want anybody to mix into her life, even in a small way. On her own she wouldn't quit, I told him, so he said he would cooperate, even if it hurt him to do it, and he fired her.

I guess it was kind of a sneaky thing to do and I'm wondering now if it was right for me to mix in. My idea was first of all to get her out of that atmosphere. She told me she had already a couple offers from nudie magazines, she turned them down of course. But some time or another, five hundred dollars for just a couple of hours work, maybe Ralphie could use a nice new suit, or he needs bail for punching a policeman, so why not? God, or his cousin Allah, gave her a beautiful figure, what's wrong to capitalize on it, like Rubinstein or

55

Picasso with their gift from heaven? If some kid wants to sit in the toilet and masturbate over the picture, this is not her business. After all, there's plenty of pictures of naked ladies hanging in the Louvre and the Uffizi and so on.

You could rationalize like this very easy, and the next step is maybe porno movies which pays even better. Doesn't matter that you started out with a strong character like this girl has certainly got. The perspective changes gradually, the black gets mixed up more and more with white, and the strong character comes out finally in saying "who gives a damn what the Establishment jerks think about it, they're only hypocrites and monsters who hide their crimes behind fancy words." I'm sure there's a lot of girls on their backs in hotel rooms with men whose names they don't know, who never started out to be call girls.

Well, I got Vangie persuaded she should try out modeling here for a while, see if she likes it. Then I had to persuade Harold it's a good idea too, we don't actually need a new model. This is a boy, you remember, who thought that somebody who is interested to make profits while people are starving in Biafra, say, or Bengal, or wherever, you never have to look far to find this terrible thing, this disgrace to God and humanity, like I say, to be interested in running a business at a profit, Harold thought you've got to be a criminal. Now, since I put him in charge, he is twice as tough about expenses and twice as anxious the business should show a profit than I ever was. Of course, I could have called him in and told him simply I want him to put Vangie on the payroll as a model. But when I made my decision to turn over the business to him to run, this is exactly what I promised myself I wouldn't do. Either he's the boss or not, I am not going to make him crazy trying to dance at two weddings with one behind.

But I didn't have with him any problem about Vangie. The appearance this girl makes, he could see right away what an asset she would be for the line, and he was not only willing but anxious.

With Larry, I got another story. I had a talk with him, T.O.T., and told him it's strictly hands off with this girl, I wouldn't stand for any nonsense from him. Well, I made it very strong but I'm still a little worried. Talk and promises are one thing and proximity is another. That's the word, no? Vangie's proximity, I could tell you, is something even I'm not immune. And Larry's proximity, I got reason to know, is not to be sneezed at. Vangie put him down good that time at the Gay Blades. But a crude pass in a nightclub is not the same as every day in the showroom, exposed to his charm, or whatever you want to call it. I've seen him turn it on and while, for me, it's got the same appeal as a hair oil commercial, with the ladies seems to be powerful stuff. You would be amazed the calls that are coming in from women in big positions, high in the fashion world, they can't wait to make fools of themselves over him. And in this case, I suppose it's a matter of pride too. Just imagine, Cary Grant would hold out his hand and say, "Come here, little girl," and he gets instead a custard pie in the face.

Well, there is a limit to how much I could concern myself. After all, what Vangie does or doesn't do is certainly more Ralphie's business than mine. Though to tell you the truth, even though I don't take too serious what she says about not wanting to get married, I don't know if this relationship has got a real future . . . No, nothing definite. Just a feeling I've got.

The big question is what am I going to do with myself. I guess it will come down to making another trip. Here too there's problems. Sophie is beginning to complain about the packing and unpacking and making connections, into airports, out of airports — last time she came back exhausted and said she needed a vacation. Me, I'm always stimulated but there's another question with travel I never thought would come up. Where? I'm running out of places.

You know the story about the customer in a travel agency who's trying to figure out a trip? The agency fellow makes him suggestions. France? Italy? Japan? Scandinavia? He's been already to these places. Germany? Very beautiful in the spring. Yes, especially around Dachau. Israel? He's been, three times. Portugal and Spain? They're fascist. Cruise? It's too boring and besides he gets seasick. Mexico? Not with his stomach. Egypt maybe, the pyramids, the Nile? Wash out your mouth. South Africa? There's not enough apartheid here? Russia? He wouldn't go near it, not only the politics but he's heard the food and the hotels are terrible and to fall into the hands of one of those Intourist girls, it's like a dentist's drill in your head all day long with the propaganda. South America maybe? Too dangerous, account of the Tupamaros and their branch offices all over.

So finally the travel man says, "Look, I'll give you a globe of the world and you can pick out some place yourself," and he goes away to wait on another customer. When he comes back he says, "Well?" and the man says, "Maybe you got another globe?"

Pretty soon this will be my situation. Listen, if you've got time, we could go somewhere, have a bite, and you could tell me what's going on with you. It's true, I don't need much encouragement, but you've got a technique to keep me talking all the time. I want to hear what *you've* got to say, for a change. Is it true the picture business in Hollywood is entirely kaput?

II

My dear friend: It's always for me a mixed pleasure to get a letter from you because you've got such a fine way to express yourself, this is a gift I would have wanted more than anything in the world, and I've got to hold myself back from talking to you like a Dutch uncle (I would like sometime to find out why Dutch uncles got especially the reputation for being strict, I had a couple of Lithuanian uncles who thought my father was too easy on me with the Hebrew lessons in the old country, I would gladly have traded them for Dutch) but like I was going to say, I want to give you lectures to stop already with the television and write something you could put on a library shelf and be proud of.

You know from long ago, when we sat on a bench in the park, talking, that I've got this special feeling about books. It's out of date now, like the rest of me. But it's hard for me to get over the feeling, when I've got a book in my hand, that I'm holding a little world that somebody created with a loan from God of the real magic in the world. To be an artist. You don't have to tell me what nonsense this is; nowadays, nine times out of ten, what you are holding in your hand is just merchandise, put together for sale, so it could just as well be TV where you get a chance for really big profits.

Anyway, it's funny you should write me just now that you are doing a show about a psychiatrist who gets mixed up with one of his lady patients and has got finally to go to a

59

psychiatrist himself. Seems to me I saw something like this already but doesn't matter, in TV the trick is to do the same thing over and over, only with a different *draydle*. Right? The main thing is you should have a signed contract and the money guaranteed, which I know I don't have to advise you; I am always surprised that a writer, a creative person, should be also good in business. I'm still a little hurt you didn't tell me when you started to buy Xerox.

What is really the funny thing about your letter, I just started myself to take from a psychiatrist. Psychoanalyst is the label he uses but it's the same box of cereal. I can hear you, there in Hollywood, saying "Seidman going to an analyst? Impossible?" Well, I got the bill right in front of me. *For professional services, March 29, April 1, 3, 5, $240.00.* Sounds like a lot of money, no? But the doctor explained to me it's part of the treatment with analysis, you must feel it's really costing you something, not like a massage or a manicure. Like with iodine, I suppose, if it doesn't hurt it's not doing you any good. But this bill I got is only after the first visit. (Session, he calls it, like it would be a meeting of Congress or something.)

I called up the doctor, it's some production to get him on the phone, when I did finally I said, "What kind of formula is it to pay a doctor in advance? In China, I read, they used to do this but then there was an understanding that you paid the doctor only when you were well, if you got sick he treated you for free."

He says, "My nurse makes up these bills on a weekly basis, if it upsets you, you can wait until you've had the subsequent sessions before you pay the bill."

"It doesn't upset me. But I'm a businessman. Suppose you would drop dead five minutes after you get my check, in advance."

60

"I've an arrangement with several of my colleagues," he says, "to take over my patients in the event of my demise."

"Suppose I don't like any of your colleagues? Will they give me the money back?"

"Mr. Seidman, I have a patient waiting. We can discuss this next time you come to the office."

"Wait a minute. Your fee is sixty dollars an hour? I heard from a couple of your graduates that you used to charge fifty."

"I'm sure you're aware of rising costs in your business too," he says.

"What do you manufacture, doctor? I understood it was just talk."

"Mr. Seidman, sixty dollars an hour is my customary fee, and has been for a couple of years. Except in hardship cases."

Well, this is all I've got to hear from him. "If I'm a hardship case," I said, "it will be *after* I'm finished with you." And I banged down the receiver. You could see I'm off to a fine start with this man. Fighting with him about money, like he would be a crook mechanic who gave me a fake estimate for a tune-up on my neurosis.

I've got to tell you how this whole thing started, with the analysis. I've been falling lately into a very bad mood. Depressed. Why? I couldn't tell you exactly. Actually, nothing has changed in my life. Except I'm retired, like I told you. I've got a birthday coming up soon, fifty-six, but physically I don't feel any different than when I was forty-six, or even thirty-six. I was never an athlete so I couldn't have a comparison to say I'm slowing up. To pull my stomach in and touch my toes twenty times, the only reaction is to get bored, like always.

I went for a checkup to my regular doctor recently. He told me I've got a constitution like a man of thirty. Heart, blood pressure, liver, prostate — the way he congratulated me on my prostate you would think I had there the Hope diamond.

"How much extra will this be on the bill?" I asked him.

He gives me a look. "What would you like, Seidman? A little myocarditis for the money? Cirrhosis of the liver? I'm sorry I can't oblige you."

"Tell me why I'm depressed," I said.

"Because you're a Democrat," he said, "and you know however much you huff and puff, that man will still be making it clear for another four years in the White House."

"What would you say if I told you I'm going to vote for him."

"I'd say get your cardiograms somewhere else from now on."

"You are really an idealist," I said. "I've got my whole faith in human nature restored."

"I know why you are depressed," he said. "Because I told you you've got nothing to worry about."

"To you," I said, "a diastolic pressure of eighty and an unswollen prostate is the answer to all the problems in the universe."

"What I wish you, Seidman," he said, "is that you should never find out how right I am. You want a prescription for some amphetamine?"

"No," I said. "And I'm not going to grow a beard, or buy a guitar either."

When I got home that evening, Sophie was on the phone with one of her club ladies. "I tried with the lentils," I heard her say. "Came out like mush." I went to the bathroom, washed my hands. When I came back Sophie was saying, "I don't think shortening from the bottom will do any good. It's got to be taken apart at the waist."

62

I went into the den, took out a book and read for ten minutes, then I went back in the living room. Sophie was saying, "I must have had on twenty pairs, every one hurt me worse than the last."

I put my hands over my ears and my luck Sophie turns around that minute and sees me. The look she gives me is not like we would be on a second honeymoon. "All right," she says in the phone, "I'll see you at the luncheon tomorrow." She puts down the receiver. "What is it with you tonight, Morris," she says to me. "You had some bad news?"

"Yes. The doctor says I could live maybe another thirty years."

"The way you are acting lately, this could be bad news for me too," she says.

"Tell me, Sophie. You are on the phone from morning to night with your club ladies. Does it ever fall into your head, any of you, that there's something going on in the world besides shoes and luncheons and you haven't got a thing to wear? Did you ever hear there's people starving by the hundreds in Pakistan?"

"I heard," she said. "And our Jewish Council just sent out two thousand food packages. What have *you* done, Mr. *Bebeck?*"

I suppose since you are practically a *goy*, you don't know what this is, a *bebeck*. But you could guess it's not a compliment, like Mr. Silver-tongued Orator. If I told you *plauderzach*, wouldn't help any, I suppose. Well, then I've got to give you a translation. Windbag, maybe. But it's not the same thing, exactly. It's more, I don't know, humorous. Windbag, you say about your neighbor's husband. *Bebeck*, you say to your own husband, and you could stay married afterward.

We start with dinner and my daughter Jenny comes in, she's dressed to go out, she just ripped a pair of gloves, has

63

Sophie got a pair to lend her. Lend her. If the Bank of America would lend on the same basis, they would be down to two branches in no time.

"Hello, Jenny," I said. "How are you this evening?"

"Hello, Pa," she says. "I'm sorry, I've got to rush."

"You look very pretty in that dress."

"Thanks," she said. "And please don't copy it. I paid for an original, I'd like to keep it that way."

She paid. I got the bill on my desk from Bergdorf, and I was trying to get up my courage to speak to her about it. $360.00 for a dress and I'm in the dress business, I mean my son is in the dress business, she could get dresses wholesale, or for free even, but this is not her style.

"Where are you going this evening?" I said.

"Out," she says. "I'll see you in the morning. 'Bye."

Well, you heard, I suppose, we've got in the country a national sickness, like in Africa encephalitis, it's called lack of communication and if I hear it one more time on the TV or read it in an article, I will start yelling and knocking my head on the wall and analysis wouldn't help anymore, they'll have to put me away. But the fact is, we got a bad case of it in the family, me and my daughter. I don't know when it started exactly. Until a couple of years ago, seems to me, we were very good friends, we would have long talks, she would come to me with problems, an advice how to handle a situation; now all I get from her is, "Please, Pa, can we *not* have a discussion about this? You just don't understand."

So make me understand? Try, at least? I'm her father, after all, not just a landlord, she owes me this much consideration, no? That's right. No. She didn't ask to be brought into the world, she's probably just an accident, anyway, and so on and so on. You've heard this story, I'm sure.

So she's out the door and I said to Sophie, "Where is she rushing?"

"She didn't tell me. You were here. Where is she rushing?"

"What's going to be with this Van Linton, Van Lipton, whatever his name is?"

"Nothing," Sophie says. "She's not seeing him anymore."

"So who is she seeing? She's not running out like this in a three-hundred-sixty-dollar dress for an orange juice at Nedick's."

"I think his name is Mamoulian," she said.

"Mamoulian. There was a movie director, very famous, by that name. This is maybe his son?"

"I don't think so. Maybe his name is Gulbenkian."

"The rug people?"

"I really don't know, Morris."

"Why don't you know? How many daughters have you got?"

"Thank God, only one."

"This is a fine attitude," I said. "What is he, an Armenian?"

"I'm not sure. I caught a glimpse of him. He looks like a foreign diplomat. Or a movie actor."

"Well, nobody could say this family is clannish. We've got a daughter-in-law who's a Presbyterian, Ralph is bringing in a Mohammedan, or an Episcopalian, you could talk to Bessie and take your choice, and maybe soon Jenny will present us with an Arabian grandchild."

"Bite your tongue," she says. "He's married."

"You're sitting there telling me our daughter is going around with a married man? You're sitting there telling me this?"

"You want me to stand up?"

65

"Sophie, it doesn't bother you that Jenny is going with a married man?"

"Suppose it bothers me. What can I do about it?"

"You could talk to her."

She gives me a pitying look, like she just found out I got softening of the brain.

Well, next day I didn't go to the shop. I waited for Jenny to come in for breakfast, about a quarter to eleven. "Hi," she says. She looks fresh as a daisy, she's a very pretty girl, my Jenny. "How do you feel?" she says.

"Rotten, thank you."

"Ma says she's trying to get you to see an analyst."

"Yes. What do you think?"

"I think you should go. You seem very down lately."

"You noticed this?"

She turns to me, with coffee in her hand. This is her breakfast, three cups of black coffee. Not even sugar. "Pa, you looking to start something with me this morning?" she says.

"What did I say?"

"You said enough to infer that I don't give a damn about how you feel. You've got the whole family upset. Talking about wills and cemetery plots — there's nothing wrong with you — "

"How do you know?"

"Dr. Landis told us. He said you're as healthy as an ox."

"From you, this is a compliment I suppose. Healthy as an ox. And just as stupid too. Maybe we should go to Luchow's to celebrate."

"Veeeery funny," Jenny says. "Why don't you do what Ma says. Find out what's bugging you."

"Maybe what's bugging me is you. Who is this man you've been seeing lately? Why haven't I been introduced to him?"

66

"You've got absolutely nothing in common. Why should you have to sit around and stare at each other, like two fish in a tank, fumbling around for something to say."

"You got a few metaphors mixed up in that speech," I said. "Maybe I could go to Berlitz and learn how to say 'what are your intentions' in Armenian?"

"Pa, if you embarrass me with this man, I swear I'll — "

"Don't tell me you'll move out, Jenny. You'll say this once too often and maybe you'll find there's a new boarder dropping her clothes all over the floor. I understand this man is married — "

"You'll have to excuse me," she says. "I've got to run. Do what Ma says. Go see Dr. Vogel."

"I always do what Ma says. For over thirty years. It brought me fame and fortune. And a daughter I can't even talk to." But she doesn't hear this; she's out the door.

Sophie gets up from the table. She's been sitting there the whole time, not saying a word. "You'll excuse me," she says, "I've got to run too."

"You got a Hadassah meeting?"

"Women For."

"I'll make a guess. *Dr.* Bernstein is speaking."

"What have you got against Dr. Bernstein suddenly. Why do you say Doctor like he would be a veterinarian or something."

"If he would be a veterinarian he'd be entitled."

"He's a Ph.D. That means *Doctor* of Philosophy, in case you haven't heard."

"I heard. And in this country a Ph.D. doesn't call himself doctor. Unless he's a faker. Isn't he the one recommended Dr. Vogel?"

"Yes. He had a very successful analysis with him himself."

"*You* say successful. I could have another opinion."

67

"All right, Morris. You do what you want. Become an old man, sitting in the park and reading those little blue books from forty years ago. One day I'm going to throw out that whole carton — "

"Just try," I said. "It'll be the first time a carton of books is the corespondent in a divorce case."

Another thing happened recently, helped to push me down a little lower. My presser, Simon, died. Funny I should say "my presser" like I would own him or something. My nephew Ralphie could make from this a big *tsimmes,* that with capitalism it's still the same old feudal system where the master owns everything and the serf owns nothing, not even his own soul. It wouldn't do any good to tell him that Simon left to his family forty units in Queens and a condominium in Florida. I remember when Harold first came in the shop, just out of the army, it was a little bit the same story. He's not a violent boy, like Ralphie, but he had his ideals and for a while he made quite a mish-mash with them in the shop. I guess a young man is not worth much if for a certain time he is not willing to get his nose bloody, finding out that you could holler from now until doomsday that all men are created equal, God or somebody has got other ideas.

It's kind of funny now, looking back, how Harold tried to get Simon to stand up for his rights and all Simon wanted to do is put in his eight hours at the pressing machine and go home to his family and his units. There's all kinds of different stars people hitch their wagons to; with Simon it was units. So now he is gone and what difference if his dream would have been Utopia, or nobody in the world should ever be hungry, or to recite all of Shakespeare by heart, or to play the violin like Heifetz. It's gone. At least the units are there and his children could be sure their children will have an education and the condominium is there for his wife to be in the sun, in Florida, with enough income to live out her years, and not have to go be a saleslady with arch-support shoes.

I said at the funeral some lines from Swinburne: "From too much love of living, from hope and fear set free, we thank with brief thanksgiving whatever gods may be, that no man lives forever; that dead men rise up never; that even the weariest river winds somewhere safe to sea."

I don't think the rabbi liked it too much that I should be quoting from an English homosexual, instead of something more kosher from the Bible.

By the way, you remember there was a misunderstanding about a Korean child that Harold adopted, with his company? I thought for a while it was a Madame Butterfly situation and I would be stuck with a grandson named maybe Kim Sung Seidman? I don't know if I told you, we sent for this boy to get his education in this country and now he is at Juilliard and he is a genius at the piano and I only wish he would be named Seidman, it would be nice to see it on a musical program instead of a dress box.

So the upshot is, I'm going to an analyst. One of the last holdouts on my block. I am not impressed with the results I see from psychoanalysis with my neighbors. I keep thinking about the joke, I still wet the bed but now I know why. Well, we'll see. It's only money. Time I've got. Too much.

I figure you are going to be interested to know how it's going with the analysis so I'm going to keep for you a record. So far I had three sessions and I couldn't see any results. I feel exactly the same. I wake up in the morning and I start to think: shower, shave, brush the teeth, comb the hair, put on the clothes, go in for breakfast, have an argument with the maid, who's got instructions from Sophie everything's got to be low cholesterol, and when I win the debate finally and get what I want it tastes anyway like straw — you know that wonderful story by Maupassant? I couldn't give it to you exactly, I read it a long time ago, but there's a young man, handsome like a god, he's standing in front of his mirror, he just got dressed for the evening, he's got a date with one of the most beautiful women in Paris, she is mad about him; tomorrow night he's also got a date with another beautiful woman, she's also crazy about him, he is the most sought after young man in Paris society, the idea he should have to spend an evening sometimes alone is out of the question, and he thinks that tomorrow night he will be standing here at the mirror putting on the finishing touches for his date with Suzette and the night after for a party at the Marquise de Recamier, and the night after at La Duchesse de Rochambeau, and the night after, another great beauty in a private booth at Maxim's — and he goes in the bathroom and takes his razor and cuts his throat.

Well, it's not the same situation but you could get an idea of my mood. I go to the office, to sit there and wait for Harold to bring me in a dress or a piece of material, I should give him a supreme court decision about the color or the style, and I've got always that same rotten feeling in the stomach, this is what I've been doing every day, year after year, and I'll go on doing it, tomorrow and tomorrow and tomorrow (is there anything ever happened to people in the world, that man Shakespeare didn't know about it?).

Then comes the other side. Here I am, fifty-five, healthy my doctor says, no financial worries, I could get up any morning and say to my wife, let's go to Yugoslavia, let's take a cruise to Tahiti, let's go take pictures of lions in Africa. Well, as you know, we had some trips, and it's fine, stimulating, but always you've got to come back and start again, getting up in the morning, to shower and shave and eat with no ap-

70

petite — the purpose is gone, you see. And what was the purpose, in the first place? The Grand Design? Something to shake the world? Or even to change it a little? An iota? The purpose was a fake, that's the realization that's in my stomach all the time, like a fatal sickness, whatever the doctor tells me about my heart and my liver and my jewel of a prostate. A fake, the whole thing. Something to keep you hypnotized, so you will stay hooked to the machinery like a robot, using up material, day in, day out — for what? To turn out a mountain of dresses that nobody needs, to feed this insanity of women who are willing every couple of years to throw out their whole wardrobes because a couple of fairies who hate them say the dresses got to be longer or shorter or long waisted or short waisted — could you believe that such a lunacy is responsible for a billion dollar business?

All right, I made money from it, lots of money, I got a nine-room apartment with a fine view of Central Park which I can see with binoculars, because to get close to it, to walk there you are taking your life in your hands; I've got a ten-thousand-dollar car, a beautiful piece of machinery that's got a schedule built in when you've got to take it to some crook and pay him two hundred dollars so it should run again — and where? Where are you going to drive a car in this city, you shouldn't go crazy from the traffic and the noise? I've got a membership in an expensive club in Westchester, I had to invent a pain in my shoulder so Harold and Sophie should stop pestering me to go there and play golf. There's some good things too, I sent my children to college (*I* say this is a good thing, is it actually, for them?), there's an established business I was able to turn over to my son so *he* could make money — and there's money to encourage my daughter to waste her life. All right, some charities. But what did I do with my own life?

I'll keep you informed, what goes on with the analyst.

You know my phonographic ear. Sometimes I wonder if it's such an advantage to have filed away in my head, like on a tape recorder, all the nonsense I had to listen to during my lifetime, and all the foolish things I said myself, and the nasty things. And always happens, when I'm feeling depressed like now, the tape gets turned on to something from maybe twenty, thirty, even forty years ago, that could still make my stomach turn over. Why is it always the shame, the guilty feeling, the humiliation that stays so strong in the memory? The compliments are all forgotten. The pleasure is like a shadow, like it happened to somebody else, or in another life. You think maybe there was another life, you get these funny flashes sometimes? That girl Vangie said something makes me think she believes in reincarnation, and she is not one of the Billie Burkes who runs to an astrologer to find out what day she should have a manicure. She is a remarkably intelligent girl. She's coming to work in the shop, by the way. I'm glad. Will be a better environment for her than that joint in New Jersey.

So here was the first session. (He's a nice-looking man, Dr. Vogel, maybe forty-five, -six, looks very serious, intelligent; I couldn't tell if he's a Jew.) He starts with a question, how old am I?

"Between fifty and seventy," I told him.

"You don't have an actual record of your birth?"

"No. I was born in Lithuania. I came here with my family when I was eight years old."

"What year was that?"

"It was the year they took the gold out of the streets and put it in Fort Knox. Nineteen-twenty-four, I think."

"That would make you fifty-five."

"Approximately. Fifty-five going on seventy."

"You mean you feel old."

"Yes."

"Why do you pick seventy as your marker for old age?"

"It's in the Bible, no? Three score and ten?"

"It's also in the Bible that Abraham begat at ninety and Methusaleh lived to be nine hundred."

"You want to play around with statistics? In Rome, two thousand years ago, the life span was twenty-six. So I've been on velvet for twenty-nine years. Except I'm not a Roman. I'm a fifty-five-year-old Jew and most of the time I feel like seventy. What is the purpose of this dialogue, at a dollar a minute?"

"I'm trying to establish that 'old' is merely a concept and has little to do with your chronological age. Churchill was in his seventies when he wrote his *History of the English-speaking Peoples*. Picasso is ninety and still hard at work. Artur Rubinstein is in his eighties — have you heard him play lately?"

"Last season."

"Did you have trouble getting seats?"

"No. I got underworld connections."

"I'm glad to hear it. I may call on you for help next time he gives a concert here. When you heard him play, did he impress you as being old?"

"He impressed me as being — I don't know — a phenomenon. A god. What are you trying to prove to me with Rubinstein and Picasso? Their life and mine. It's two different species, a dress manufacturer and a great artist. Like — I don't know — an antelope and a frog."

"You have no sense of achievement, Mr. Seidman?"

"Well, I achieved to give my children a college education. I achieved to get for my wife an apartment on Central Park West and a full-time maid. I achieved to get for the maid a

73

color television for her room and a portable Sony for the kitchen that she can keep on all day long and drive us crazy. And once, in nineteen-fifty-four, I got a nice letter from the Central Hanover Bank, how much they appreciated my pre-paying the interest on a note. This is more or less an inventory of my achievement."

"I see," he says. I could feel he's studying me from in back, maybe the shape of my head, to see if he could tell something about what kind of a nut he is dealing with here.

"Oh yes," I said. "Something else. I achieved lately to get a girl fired from a topless joint in New Jersey and gave her a job as a model in my place. My son's place, I mean. Where I still got a courtesy office."

He waits for me to go on. I got nothing more to say so I wait. Finally he says, "Is there anything else you want to tell me about this girl?"

"There's nothing to tell. She's a beautiful girl, she's interested in archaeology and she's sleeping with my nephew. Maybe they will get married."

Again he waits. I wait. "Anything else?" he says.

"About what?"

No answer. He's making me very nervous with this technique. "Mr. Seidman," he says, "why do you feel you need analysis?"

"Who said I feel I need it? My wife feels I need it."

"Do you always let your wife make your decisions?"

"Are you married, doctor?"

"Yes."

"How long?"

"Twenty-one years."

"I got you beat by a few years. Maybe you also decided, sometime after the honeymoon, that it's not worth while to win arguments with your wife, when she gets a fixed idea

74

in her head? Does a person have to be a mental case for this? Henpecked? Castrated, maybe?"

"I haven't made any judgments about you, Mr. Seidman," he says. "That's not my function. I'm here to help you define your problems, understand them, come to grips with them. At the moment, I'm trying to get at your motivation in coming to see me."

"I'll make it simple for you," I said. "I figure it's cheaper for me to pay your bill than to get a divorce. Incidentally, if I could speak freely — "

"Please do. That's what you're here for."

"Well, I don't like to insult people — "

"When my patients start insulting me, Mr. Seidman, I begin to feel I'm getting somewhere with them."

"You hit the jackpot with me, doctor. This is a pretty broken-down couch for a man who makes your kind of money."

"I haven't furnished my office to impress anyone," he says. "The idea is for my patients to feel relaxed, at ease. At home."

"If you want me to feel at home," I said, "you'll have to get a new couch. At home I've got in my den a beautiful French provincial, with special upholstery and a triangle pillow for my head. And on the walls I've got, besides books, a couple of very nice originals we bought in Paris, not cheap reproductions of Dufy and Utrillo, every grocery store has got them now and even my sister Bessie wouldn't hang them up in her house."

"You sound cranky, Mr. Seidman," he says. "Do you have any idea why?"

"I've got a very good idea why," I said. "And why do you say cranky? You think I don't know the word hostile?"

"It's too soon for me to know what you know, Mr. Seidman," he says. "Or what you think you know." It's a nice little dig, but polite, and I had it coming, I have to admit. "If you prefer the word, why are you feeling hostile?" he says.

"Because I figure it's going to cost me seven, eight hundred dollars a month to come here and *hock a tchynik* — "

"Does that mean 'talk aimlessly'?"

"Fine. I'm going to have to translate too. What is it, doctor, you're a Gentile?"

"Would it bother you if I were?"

"What bothers me," I said, "is that I've got a writer friend, I've been talking my head off to him for years, he doesn't charge me a cent, he sends me presents instead, and autographed copies of his books."

"You feel it does you good to talk to him?"

"Yes."

"Then why don't you go talk to him instead of me?"

"Because my wife wants me to talk to you. On account of there's a certain Mr. Bernstein, who is a Ph.D. in fund-raising, at fifteen percent for himself, took from you for a few years and from being a mixed-up faker and phony he is now an adjusted faker and phony, and a big man on the Hadassah circuit. And my wife, God bless her, is very impressed with him. I don't know if you've got him on a commission basis but every time he comes to the house, there's a big commercial for psychoanalysis, particularly the Dr. Vogel brand. Between my wife and my daughter, they wore me down finally. So I'm here. And my writer friend is in Hollywood, working for TV. He's writing a show about a psychiatrist who is a bigger screwball than any of his patients."

"The idea pleases you, doesn't it?"

"Doesn't please me, doesn't displease me. I think it's kind of a funny idea. I'll tell you this, doctor, frankly, there's quite a few people in our neighborhood, besides Bernstein, who got diplomas from you and I don't look forward when I've got to meet them for a social evening. Maybe they feel fine but an evening with them is for me no pleasure. They are the biggest *noodnicks* in the world."

"What does that mean?"

"You analyzed half the people on Central Park West and you don't know what *noodnick* means?"

"I want to know what it means to you."

"It means a person who thinks his life story is more interesting than Dostoevski's *Idiot,* only he hasn't got time to write it. But he's got all the time in the world to talk it, and if you fall asleep, listening, the conclusion he comes to is not that he put you to sleep, but that either you've got some kind of brain damage, or you had too much to drink before dinner."

"In other words, to put it somewhat more briefly, a bore."

"Why do you want to be brief, doctor? You lose money that way. Listen," I said, "do I have to lie on this couch? It makes me nervous. Couldn't I sit up?"

"Of course. If that suits you better."

"I prefer it. As long as I'm here, I would rather talk to you than to the ceiling."

"Fine. But try to remember that I'm here to help you understand yourself and your problems, not as your opponent in a verbal chess game."

"Do you mind if I make a personal comment, doctor?"

"You haven't been exactly impersonal so far. Go ahead."

"You sounded a little cranky to me, just now."

"You mean, hostile?"

"No. Cranky. Irritable."

"I wasn't aware of it," he said. "Would you like me to be cranky with you?"

77

"Doesn't make any difference," I said. "Wouldn't change my opinion about anything."

"What is your opinion?"

"I think you are a snake oil salesman. Not just you. Your whole profession."

"Wouldn't racket be closer to what you mean?"

"I'm trying to be polite."

"Don't. Try to be honest. Are these honest statements you've been making? Honest opinions? Or are you just trying to irritate me?"

"Well, let me think. Yes. I think so. I'm trying to irritate you."

"Why?"

"Because you irritate me. The way you keep on with the questions, like I would be a cockroach you're turning around and giving little jolts to see which one of the legs twitches."

"That's an odd evocation. Are you thinking, by any chance, about a story by Kafka called 'Metamorphosis'?"

I didn't realize before but the minute he said it, I knew that was what was in my mind, in the back.

"Maybe I was thinking about it," I said.

"That would fit in with your feeling of depression. Of worthlessness."

"Yes. I suppose so . . . It's a terrible story."

"You mean terrifying."

"Yes. Terrifying."

"Let's go back a bit," he says. "It's my job to keep a certain detachment with my patients but it's not impossible that you could irritate me. I'm not a machine and you're very good with the needle."

"I should be, no? I've been in the needle trade all my life."

"May I remind you that you'd be paying a very high price for the petty satisfaction of getting a rise out of me."

78

"Don't worry about the price. I could afford it."

"But I'm afraid I can't. You see, there's a premium on my time. There are just so many hours in the day and I've got a waiting list. Believe it or not, one of my principal motivations in doing what I do is a desire to help people. I could be using this time for a patient with a real problem. Who wants to be helped."

"Isn't this a real problem, doctor? A man who is willing to spend sixty dollars an hour just to needle you?"

He bites the end of a finger, looking at me.

"Did you suck your thumb when you were a child, doctor?" I ask him.

He takes his finger out of his mouth, looks at it, then, "Mr. Seidman," he says, "why are you afraid of analysis?"

"Aha," I said. "The game."

"What do you mean, the game?"

"The people with the diplomas. Your ex-patients. They've got a game they play when they get together. This is how you know they belong to the club. Who is scared of women because he is always jumping up to light their cigarettes? Who is hostile toward analysis, and sneers at it, because he's afraid of what he would find out about himself if he took some? Who wants to smash every fairy in the face because he's really one himself, doesn't matter how many women he goes to bed with? Who hates his mother because he calls her every day on the phone? — well, I'll tell you right off, doctor, I've got the worst symptoms. I wish I could call my mother every day on the telephone, maybe twice a day, and send her flowers every week instead of once a year to the cemetery. I don't want to smash any fairies, I am not a smasher by nature, but I am good and sick of how much influence they've got today in art and fashion and the theater. I am very annoyed when I pay twelve dollars for a ticket and I've got to sit and listen to their twisted ideas

79

and their humor that's got needles sticking out everywhere — I could recognize it immediately and it turns my stomach."

"You know there are scholars who believe they've got proof that Shakespeare was a homosexual."

"Listen, if somebody writes like Shakespeare, he could be an Arab, even. But anyway, we are making very good progress, no? I've been here half an hour and already we've got established that I had a fixation on my mother and there's a good suspicion I'm a latent homosexual, the way I talk about them, and the reason I am hostile with you is because I really want to have an affair with you. At this rate we could be through with my whole analysis in two sessions and I'm pleading with you, doctor, don't graduate me. Let's spend the hour playing pinochle or something, because I promised my wife I would take from you for at least three months."

He doesn't say a word. He just sits there. Maybe he's thinking about his income tax. So I figure two can play this game and I just sit there too, until after a while he says, "What are you thinking, Mr. Seidman?"

"I was thinking," I said, "that maybe it wouldn't be so quick with the analysis, after all."

"What changed your mind?"

"Well, I'm looking at you now and I couldn't see you as a father figure."

"What makes you think you have to?"

"Isn't this the theory in psychoanalysis? You are supposed to be a father figure and I am supposed to get a transference so I could work out what my emotional problems were when I was a child. But the trouble is, to be my father you would have to be about eighty, and much skinnier, with a worried look on your face. I figure you to be about forty-five, which

gives me a whole mixed-up feeling because if I was precocious like my nephew Ralphie, I could be *your* father instead. And if I am supposed to start having dreams about
you, it's true that you would be about the right age of my
father when he died, but even in a dream I couldn't see
you as a man who operates a pushcart and loses money every
week on the overhead."

I don't know if he laughed, or coughed. "Mr. Seidman,"
he said, "why don't you forget your preconceptions about
analysis. Apart from your somewhat garbled, if entertain-
ing, notions, what you're talking about is deep analysis,
which I wouldn't dream of going into with you. At your
age — I mean your chronological age — it would be a dubi-
ous investment of time and money. Besides, I don't think
it's indicated. You're not that troubled. I think a few
sessions of frank talk might give you some insight into your
present mood, and a fresh perspective on the time remain-
ing to you. But that's up to you. I don't need the business.
If you're determined not to let me help you, I'd appreciate
it if you'd quit now, and go play golf."

"You too, doctor? One thing I beg you, let there be one
person at least who is not sending me to play golf, for heav-
en's sake."

"Then suppose you stop fending me off and let's try to
find out what's really causing your depression."

"All right, but I got to tell you what's bothering me about
being here, and it's not hostility or because I'm afraid I got
something terrible hidden in my subconscious; we are all
murderers, doctor, we got our inheritance from the wolves
and hyenas, and we made some improvements over claws
and sharp teeth in a few million years. I don't need analysis
to know this. But it's true I'm self-conscious about coming
here to complain about my problems when there's maybe a

81

billion people in the world who got up this morning not knowing if they'll have what to eat, or which one of their children is maybe going to die of sickness or malnutrition, and there's nobody to give a damn about them, or if a bomb is going to be dropped on them by some nice young man, could be my son or your son, who is trying to preserve their freedom.

"And here I am, I woke up this morning in a fine apartment on Central Park West, the breakfast I pushed away from me that got thrown in the garbage would be a feast for those families that they'll never see in their whole lives. I got a profitable business, I don't have to lift a finger anymore, my son runs it brilliantly — if you could use a word like this for the dress business — he's married to a beautiful girl, he wrote her some very nice poems before they got married and now she maybe needs a little psychiatric help herself because she doesn't hate her in-laws, in fact my wife and I have got to make excuses sometimes not to have her invite us so often, for her part we would be seeing them twice a week, and on Sundays besides, you've got to admit this is kind of peculiar, some kind of neurosis, no?"

"Maybe she's perfectly normal and enjoys your company, Mr. Seidman. Have you considered that possibility?"

"Anybody enjoys my company these days couldn't be normal."

"Tell me about the rest of your family."

"Well, I've got a darling grandchild who wears me out reading to her, maybe in that little mind is a seed that is going to grow into a wonderful talent, an Emily Dickinson, or maybe a Guiomar Novaes, she is pretty advanced already on the piano. I've got my own daughter who's bright and pretty — I worry sometimes that she will find out one day what Santayana says, that life is not a spectacle or a feast,

82

only a dilemma, and that she wouldn't be prepared for this discovery. But to me she is more of a person than any of the daughters of our friends; she reads a book sometimes at least and I think she's got talent as an artist."

"That's your family? Two children."

"Yes."

"And your wife?"

"She could still make people sit up and take notice when we walk into a theater or a restaurant. And she still thinks she loves me, don't ask me why. And the upshot is, I'm depressed. Why? Because I've got another day to get through. Like it would be a prison sentence, and I'll tell you the truth, sometimes I think what a blessing it would be for me if I would have a heart attack, quick, and finished with the whole business. This is the story, and you figure it out."

"What's important, Mr. Seidman, is for *you* to figure it out. If we're going to get anywhere, we're going to have to speak very frankly, and openly. You understand that."

"What have I been doing?" I said. "You couldn't accuse me of making you compliments like an Arabian diplomat."

"I want to ask you frankly," he says, "if you think your present feeling of depression has anything to do with sex."

"What do you mean?" I said. "You want to know if I think sex is depressing? The answer is no. On the contrary."

"I mean, do you have any feelings of inadequacy at this point?"

"Depends," I said. "How many times a night is inadequate?"

"Stop fencing with me, Mr. Seidman. You know what I'm talking about."

"Well, I don't know how to answer you," I said. "I couldn't honestly say it falls into my head to go home in the

83

afternoon and say to my wife, 'Sophie, take your clothes off.' But I'll tell you the truth, even twenty years ago if I would have done this I think she would have sent for a doctor, or maybe the police."

"What I'm getting at," he says, "is whether you feel there's been any significant diminution of your libido, your sexual drive."

"Again I don't know how to answer this question, doctor. I think my trouble is there's been a significant diminution of my drive for everything. Not just sex."

"Why did you give up active participation in your dress business?"

"I don't know exactly. It was a happening, like they say now. I started to do some traveling, turned over some responsibility to my son, he handled everything fine, we went away for another trip and this way, gradually, it slipped away from me, the whole thing. I shouldn't say slipped; I dropped it because I lost interest, I was only too glad to let it go. Maybe to see the Winged Victory at night in the Louvre, and a whole roomful of paintings by Goya in the Prado — maybe this had something to do with it. Maybe it was a big mistake for me to take time to think, to see what people can do with their lives."

"You still go down to your place of business every day?"

"Yes. I got a nice room there, outside view, a nurse who can also type, she makes me coffee, answers the phone, my son gives me some occupational therapy, a book of swatches to look at, some letters to sign and so on."

"But generally speaking your son actually runs the business."

"Generally speaking."

"And you're satisfied with this arrangement."

"I see what you're driving at, doctor. Since I told you I

84

hate the dress business, and according to Freud every son is hostile to his father and vice versa, this is a way I figured out to get Harold trapped in the business and let *him* break his head over it for the next thirty years."

"Mr. Seidman, I thought we were going to dispense with this kind of thing. It's just wasting time and costing you money."

"Relax, doctor," I said. "I could afford the money and the hour I've got to spend with you anyway, three times a week, that's the contract. So I could go home afterward and tell my wife I had a good session with you and she won't *noodjeh* me."

"That means 'nag you'?"

"Listen, are you a Gentile or aren't you? Why does it have to be a mystery?"

"I'm a Jew, Mr. Seidman. But I was born in Germany and that's the language I grew up with. Yiddish wasn't spoken in my home."

"I know. It's only spoken by the lower classes of Jews. My experience is German Jews got a snobbish feeling about Russian Jews. How's it with your experience?"

"I've heard that. In my own case, I was away from home — in school in Switzerland — when my parents were packed into a cattle car and shipped to Auschwitz where they were gassed. That was in Poland. I doubt they had much chance to exercise their snobbery there."

Well, this shut me up pretty good for a minute. I felt sick in my stomach and very much ashamed. "Listen, doctor," I said, "what I'm saying here about your profession and so on, it's nothing personal. I'm sure there's people, you do them some good. But I don't see what you could do for me, unless you got a potion to make me twenty years younger and pull the wool back over my eyes again so I wouldn't see that everything is, like it says in Ecclesiastes, vanity and a striving after wind."

"Everything, Mr. Seidman?"

"Everything. You've got to ask me? After your parents were gassed by the Nazis? When you are young, you are hypnotized, drunk, I don't know what. You dream. Then comes a day when you wake up and you see the nighttime, the real nighttime of the world, and it's finished. You can't fool yourself anymore about what's what. Auschwitz is the real thing. This is what life is. Everything else is fakery. Painkillers."

"What about your feeling for your son. Your daughter. Your wife. All fakery?"

"It's an instinct, what I feel for my son and daughter. A goony bird feels the same thing. I keep thinking about it. Who are they, Harold and Jenny? I don't really know them. Who knows anybody, actually? I love the children, and my grandchild, maybe even more. That's what I say. But what does it mean? When they please me I love them. When they don't please me I stop loving them. It's all nonsense, sham, this talk about love. Nobody loves anybody. Maybe General Motors loves the banks which are lending them money."

"And your wife? You think her concern for you is a fake?"

"Poor Sophie. Or maybe lucky Sophie. She's still hypnotized. Disturbs her that I'm depressed. I mope, she says, and this bothers her because in her eyes I am still the young man she married, full of hopes and dreams and ambitions; she would like to think I'm the same person. So she sends me to have an analysis to find out why I mope, and she feels better. She wants to call this love? Let her live and be well with it. Vanity, saith the Preacher. Vanity of vanities. All is vanity."

"And I'm a fake too?" he says.

86

"Of course. But you are an honest fake. You're still dreaming. You think what you're doing has got some reason to it. Like I thought there was a reason for me to work twelve hours a day and eighteen on weekends, with the worrying thrown in, to be a success in the dress business. I suppose there are people who live and die like this, still dreaming. I envy them. I hope it won't happen to you some day to wake up and realize that what you are doing is all nonsense."

"You think it's nonsense to alleviate suffering?"

"No. This is the only thing that people could do. *Against* the nonsense. But how often, doctor, do you really alleviate? And for every one there's a hundred new ones climbing the walls and screaming for help no one can give them. Listen, it's an old story, what I'm telling you. You want to get it in beautiful language, read it sometime in the Bible. Ecclesiastes. 'All things are full of labor, man cannot utter it. All the rivers run into the sea, yet the sea is not full.' Beautiful, doctor, and terrible when you realize. You think he could have used an analysis, that fellow?"

"Well, we have to stop now, Mr. Seidman," he says. "I'll see you on Wednesday."

This afternoon I got a call from Miss Elkins; I was on my way to get my care and drive uptown, and I saw Vangie by the elevator. She was wearing a granny dress and the hair tied back from her head in a pigtail.

"You are a remarkable girl, Vangie," I told her. "Just before, in the showroom, when you were modeling number one-twenty-four, you looked like you were ready to sit down for dinner with Henry Kissinger and fourteen ambassadors to the U.N. Now you look like a schoolgirl."

She gave me a smile and I thought, this Ralphie, if he's got anything to him besides the three piece set in his pants and his talent for getting into trouble, with a girl like this to inspire him he's got to become Attorney General at least.

"You're going to school now?" I said.

"Yes. I've got my classes arranged for three mornings and two afternoons. It's working out fine. I'm very grateful. But I do feel as if I'm taking advantage."

"You're not, but suppose you would be. So take advantage. It gives me pleasure. I mean, it gives my son and me pleasure. After all, what good is a business if you can't give your family a little advantage? You might just as well be a politician and give away all your money to the poor. You're getting along all right with Harold?"

"Oh yes. He's very nice. He's got all your consideration and charm."

"And thank God, his mother's looks and brains." We were in the street now and I said, "I'm going for my car. You want to drive uptown with me? Takes longer but it's still nicer than the subway."

"I've got plenty of time," she said. "My Spanish class isn't until two."

"You're taking Spanish? This is for Mexico? Yucatán?"

"Yes."

"You're really serious about the archaeology."

"Very serious."

"More than Ralphie?"

"Mr. Seidman, we've been over that." She gives me again a smile but this time it told me exactly where to get off. I can't tell you how much I admire this girl, how she handles things.

I gave the boy my ticket for the car. "You're sure I won't be taking you out of your way," she said.

"No. I'm going to visit my girl friend, it's not far from your school." I was looking to see her reaction. She jerked

88

her head around to look at me. "You're surprised I've got a girl friend?"

"No," she says. "Not at all." Of course. Wouldn't fit for a modern young woman to think there is anything wrong that a man of fifty-five, married, should have a girl friend. Why not? Man is a polygamous animal, marriage is an unnatural institution, etcetera and so forth. But I could see she was surprised.

The boy brought up the car, I got in with her and started up.

"Tell the truth, Vangie," I said. "You didn't think I was the type."

"I don't think of people as types," she said. "Just people."

"But if it was Larry, would seem more natural to you, no?"

"Oh, Larry," she said. "He's a joke."

"There's women could tell you this joke ends up with tears."

"Come on, Mr. Seidman," she said. "You can't seriously think Larry's a threat to anyone but an aging career woman who's begun to count her orgasms."

I nearly bumped the car in front of us. You see, with this girl, if you are not prepared for a straight answer you better not open up the subject. Maybe *you* are surprised I would take her into my confidence on such a personal matter. After all, it's not something you mention to everybody, that you've got a girl friend. Maybe I had an ulterior motive. The analyst is always looking for them. If I say to him the simplest thing, like for instance I had oysters Rockefeller for lunch, pretty soon he will be asking me if I eat them often and if I think they are good for my sex life and sixty dollars later — or maybe three hundred and sixty; this kind of treasure hunt could go on for six sessions — and a peculiar thing, from starting out yelling "for Christ's sake, I *like* oysters

89

Rockefeller, what kind of a *tsimmes* are you trying to make out of it," I end up actually wondering if maybe I am worried about getting impotent, and if the reason I criticized Jenny's appearance this morning is because she was out with her Armenian boy friend last night, who looks like a stud, and like a movie actor besides.

Well, in this case I did have an ulterior motive, I admit. What it is, I love to hear this girl talk. We covered already a pretty wide range of subjects. Gloria Steinem, that Greek philosopher, what's his name, begins with an A, not Aristotle, oh yes, Agnew; we discussed Mrs. Mitchell, she should live and be well, in Europe maybe, or South Africa; we've talked about music, the theater, movies — she likes theater better than movies — and *Playboy,* she thinks it's a very good magazine, better even than the old *Police Gazette,* and the *Playboy* philosophy, she thinks, should be taught in schools, in the third grade, and so on.

I love to watch the expressions on her face when she's thinking about an answer to give me, or she's getting ready to give me a dig — after all, I'm still the older generation, the Establishment. But it's never that I'm the Enemy, like with Ralphie. Or if I am, I got my ammunition blown up, and my guns put out of commission long ago. She loves to laugh — to hear her is altogether a musical experience — and she thinks I'm funny. Well, if you can't be Cary Grant, or Heifetz, it's something at least to be funny.

The main thing is, I value getting her opinion about things. It's an education for me. This is her world, after all, where she and Jenny and all the young people live, and to me it's a foreign country. No, this is not a good way to express it. Because I enjoy to go to foreign countries, it's a challenge for me to learn a little bit of the customs and the language, to make myself understood. But here, I feel only confused and sad and irritated most of the time. Because, after all, it's not foreigners you are dealing with, who have got their own life and you've got yours, soon you will go home and if you enjoyed what you experienced, fine, and if not, next time you'll go somewhere else. These are your own, your children, or your friends' children, you can't just be an onlooker, a tourist, you feel some way responsible. And always frustrated, what's really going on in their hearts and minds. Are they really as selfish as they seem? As dopey? Have they really got nothing in their minds but to hate you and wait for you to get out of the way, to die?

I noticed my daughter lately has got a technique with me, in fencing it's called parry. Actually, I suppose she doesn't want to hurt me, so she just turns aside everything I say that could bring us maybe to some understanding. "Veeeery funny," is her favorite expression. Or, "You're right, Pa, you're absolutely right, so let's not discuss it anymore." Or, "Can we turn the record over, Pa, I've heard this side until it's coming out of my ears." Period. End of paragraph. End of discussion.

And the young people you see sometimes on the TV, they get them together for a panel discussion about drugs, sex, politics, after two minutes listening I get so nervous, I've got to go take a Valium. That lingo. "Like wow, man, you people blew it, man, y'know, I'm telling it like it is, man, y'know, like wow."

Like, y'know, these kids would have a deal with some enemy planet to destroy first the language and afterward, y'know, will be only numbers, nobody will have to waste time making, y'know, sentences, or take time off from passing around the Jefferson Airplanes, just pick a number from one to thirteen and peace, man, like wow.

But this girl, Vangie, is a person with a brain not doped

91

up with pot or drugs, she's got a fine vocabulary and a respect for a beautiful, rich language, and for education in general; she's got a philosophy, for sure it's different than mine, maybe so different I will never really understand it, but it's a pleasure to talk to her, to get her views. To exchange ideas. Where did it go, this wonderful parlor game?

Anyway, I said, "I'm entitled, right? A girl friend. A man married thirty-three years?"

"You're sure you want to discuss this with me?" she says.

"Sure, I'm sure. Who else? The golf pro at my club? Larry?"

She doesn't smile. "When you talk about being married for thirty-three years and what that entitles you to," she says, "you make it sound as if you've served a sentence, paid your debt to society and now you're entitled to act like a free man. You were entitled to do that any time, married or not."

"This is how you would feel about a husband? No demands? No restrictions?"

"I can't know how I'd feel about a husband. I haven't had one and I don't intend to. But if I did, I'd certainly hope that my female genes, or whatever, aren't hung up on the kind of lousy possessiveness that's built into Christian marriage."

"Genes are not hung up on attitudes, Vangie. You should know that from your studies."

"You mean the Lamarckian bit."

"Yes. The Russians had one too, Lysenko. Tried to prove, I guess, that you could produce crops of born Communists, like potatoes. The real scientists say that genes are only programmed with survival things, from evolution. But the past has still got some kind of hold on us, some value. Customs, traditions — "

92

"And that means we have to accept them all, respect them all? We'd still be having human sacrifice if somebody, sometime, didn't have the sense and the guts to say No, this tradition stinks."

"You got a very good point, Vangie. But does it mean that with each new generation, *everything* should be thrown away? Some customs have got survival value too. If you see something that's lasted thousands of years, you've got to think there's something to it, more than just habit. Marriage, the idea, goes back so many thousands of years. It's not even just Christian, or Jewish, to have strict ideals about sex — "

"Let's say strict prejudices."

"All right, but so far as I could see, it's a universal thing. Take that Indian god in Mexico, Quetzal something — "

"Quetzalcohuatl."

"Yes. Either he was a man-god or a god-man, I couldn't figure out but anyway he was pure, like Galahad and Adonis, and his enemy — I can't say his name either — "

"Texcatlipoca. God of Night."

"Well, this god of night was jealous of Quetzal's purity, so one night he made him very drunk and fixed him up with a girl to sleep with — "

"It was his sister, in most of the legends."

"That's like Greek already. Anyway, the next morning when Quetzal woke up and saw the girl and he knew he wasn't pure anymore, he went to the ocean near Veracruz and burned himself up and became a star. This is the story, no? From the Aztec bible."

"There is no Aztec bible. There are only some accounts put together by priests at the time of the Conquest, probably slanted. But the Quetzalcohuatl legend runs through almost all the Indian cultures in Mexico."

"So it shows they put a big value on this kind of purity. Maybe they didn't live like this themselves, just like us, but they had the ideal. Why? If it's only a foolish prejudice."

"That's a good question. I'll bring it up in my archaeology class. Why didn't you give me a clue you were interested in Mexican mythology, you remarkable man?"

"*You* got me interested. I just started to read about it lately. It's pretty confusing, you know. Those names. And it's like everybody's got a different idea about where and what and how, and they all come to different conclusions. But it's fascinating, the whole subject. Long ago I read a book, Fraser's *Golden Bough* — "

"That's the Old Testament," she says. I could see she's got a gleam in her eyes, this is her love, this subject, "the library's bulging with commentaries since. You know, archaeology has its Talmud too. And Talmudists. They love nothing better than to gather round and braid inferences into conjecture, or vice versa, and end up miles away from the pottery shard that started the whole thing."

"How is it going with the real Talmud, by the way?"

"Well, I've learned how to make potato pancakes." She gives a little laugh, I wish I could describe the sound, it's so much part of her style.

I said, "I don't think this was what my sister had in mind when she introduced you to the rabbi. How old is he, Vangie?"

"About thirty. And very attractive."

"What does Ralph think about him?"

"I don't know. I haven't asked him. Tell me about your girl friend."

"I'll do better. We could make a stop and I'll introduce you, if you've got time. I think she would enjoy to meet you."

94

"You think that's — er — "

"Discreet? I trust you, Vangie. Besides, in these modern days, who cares actually? What is sex? An appetite, like other appetites. Right? Who says you got to eat always in the same restaurant. And the same menu. I worked hard all my life. I could afford some caviar now."

"And champagne," she said. "This car runs like kicking a pillow downhill."

"Don't change the subject," I said. "Actually, you don't approve of my having a girl friend."

"Why do you say that?"

"I've got radar. You are flashing me signals. Or maybe what you don't approve of is my talking about it."

"I think you're trying to be honest," she said, "and I certainly approve of that. But I don't think my approval or disapproval is relevant."

"You could do me a big favor, Vangie, and find some other word, not relevant. I'm so sick of it, from the TV. Last year it was meaningful. Meaningful dialogue. I could vomit when I hear it. Maybe this is why the kids get in the habit to talk like zombies."

"Maybe," she said.

"But 'Y'know, man, tell it like it is, man, right on, man' — over and over — is that better?"

"We were talking about caviar and sex," she said.

"And I think you don't like the idea somebody should put them together, like luxuries you got to pay a high price for."

"I don't think you should have to pay for sex."

"You mean me? Or anybody?"

"I mean anybody, of course. But especially not you."

"What about an apartment, clothes, a servant, utilities — "

"Well, it's one-sided at this juncture, I admit. But that's what you do for a wife, isn't it?"

"For a wife it's not paying. It's something you want to do because — well, because this is what love is."

"Ah love," she says. "Now we're into something heavy."

"You mean, like a statue of Aphrodite, fished up from the sea."

"Well, it's illuminating to hold your little fancies and prejudices up to time and see the holes. That's healthy."

"You think a good Catholic or Muslim would say it's healthy?"

"I don't know. What about a good Jew?"

"I couldn't tell you. I'm not a good Jew. But healthy or not, to lose the authority, the certainty — like Jehovah is maybe not all powerful, or Allah is maybe not so merciful — and love is maybe an illusion altogether — doesn't this make life pretty confusing?"

"Uh huh," she said. "Dangerous too. Like falling in love with Henry the Eighth. You think what he called falling in love is a hell of a lot different than what a sex murderer calls it?"

"It's true he was kind of a monster but think how this man turned the world upside down so he could get married to a girl he wanted. Why? Because, however much he was the king, who could do what he wants, he was still afraid of some judgment on him. And he wanted a son born legitimate. What is legitimate? Only a word. Like marriage. Love. Sin. I'll tell you something, Vangie. I think we all want to sin and we need religion to say what sin is. Not mainly because of the idea of forbidden fruit but because if there's no sin and no rules and anything we do is okay, then the world is suddenly empty and life has got absolutely no meaning, even to ourselves, and this is the most terrible idea of all."

She was looking at me, the eyes a little smoky, thinking.

96

"Okay," she said, "but then it comes down to what your religion is and what you think sin is. For me it's pretty clear. Sin is hurting people, deceiving them, humiliating them. Maybe ignoring them. And that's it. I don't need to populate the world with a lot of school principals holding up signs saying 'Thou Shalt Not' in order not to feel alone and shivery in the universe."

"Well, we are getting in pretty deep for a ride uptown," I said. "We've got to spend an evening together — "

It came out without my even thinking about it and I stopped.

"Right on," she said. "And soon." I saw there was a little mischief in her eyes now. "You'll have a bit of juggling to do between your girl friend and your wife."

"No problem," I said. "I'm an accomplished liar. I've been doing it for years. But, seriously, you think it's all right that I should have a girl friend. Even if I've got to be sneaky about it."

"Well, I don't like the word sneaky — "

"The word? Or the idea?"

"Both. But I suppose, in these circumstances, you could do some fancy footwork and end up with 'discreet,' which has nicer connotations. You wouldn't have to, of course, if it weren't for our stupid puritan heritage."

"You mean, talmudic heritage."

"Okay. Both."

"But basically you approve."

"If it matters, yes. I told you, I think the idea of people possessing each other, or thinking they've a right to, is an abomination. Everyone should be free to decide what he needs and wants — "

"A beautiful theory. But who is lucky enough to know what he really needs and wants. And then how to get it. And then who he has to step on to get it. That's sometimes a problem too. You said your religion is not to hurt anybody."

"That's right. I think it's yours too. I'm sure you wouldn't deliberately hurt anybody to get anything," she said.

"Well, I hope so. But who knows? This girl just came along. It happened."

"I understand. Completely."

"You wouldn't let on anything to anybody? Harold, especially." She gave me a very funny look. I made out I didn't see it. "Harold thinks all I need is more golf. If only I would concentrate on making my left arm and my wrist and the club one straight line when I swing, my problems would fall away from me like drops from an old oaken bucket. I would love myself, and my neighbors, the burned forests near the DMZ would be green again, all the babies would stop crying and God would be back in his heaven, counting sparrows instead of North Vietnamese bodies. So when I leave the shop like this I tell Harold I'm going to the club. He's getting to be an old fogy too. Thirty-two. Why should I upset him?"

She didn't say anything, just moved her mouth a little like she was going to, and then decided she wouldn't. I wondered if maybe I went too far with this game. Actually, she looked kind of upset. Well, not upset, who am I to her, after all, to upset her, what I do or don't do. Maybe a little uncomfortable is a better description. Like I opened for her a door where she doesn't want to go in.

I turned off Park Avenue into 125th and she said, "I don't think I should stop to meet your girl friend."

"Why?"

"Well, she might not appreciate it. She might have some ideas of her own about my intruding on her privacy."

"No, believe me, she will appreciate it. She doesn't get

98

much chance to meet people. Not that I keep her a prisoner. But — you understand."

"Yes. Of course."

When we walked into the clinic, everybody gave me a big hello. Why not? They know how their bread gets buttered. Miss Elkins, the head nurse, came up to me and said, "I'm glad you could make it, Mr. Seidman. Edna is terrified."

"And otherwise?"

"The vital signs are good. But — " She pushed out her hands.

"But wouldn't hurt if the morale was better," I said.

"Exactly."

"This is Miss Jamison," I said. "She works for me. And she goes to school at Barnard. Near here."

I don't know why I had to give her this history. I got to stop apologizing to people for being alive, once and for all.

"How do you do," Miss Elkins said and right away I knew this girl is too pretty for her taste. She is a fine, compassionate woman, Miss Elkins, but the time she is at her best is with someone who's a poor thing, sick, and if ugly too is even better.

We went to the second floor and Vangie stopped to look at the plaque. *In Memory of Rebecca Seidman, 1896–1934.*

"She was my mother," I told her. "She died from uremic poisoning when she was thirty-eight. It's from bad kidneys. They couldn't do anything about it then. Now there's a machine for washing the blood. When I got so I could afford it, I donated one here and they put up this tablet and they gave me the privilege to be a fund raiser for the clinic. I don't like to ask people for money so I'm a fund raiser mostly from myself. Costs me plenty."

We went into one of the rooms where Edna was lying in

a bed behind a screen. She was dopey, half asleep, but when she saw me she tried to sit up and held out her arms to me. Is there anything nicer to see than a person's face who is really glad to see you? Especially a person about eleven years old, with a thin face and big eyes, that already got half the pain and sorrow of the world in them. I gave her a hug and said, "What is going on, Edna? Tell me."

"I'm going to die," she said. "I wanted to see you before."

"I'm sorry to disappoint you," I said. "I mean, everybody is going to die but you got to wait about seventy years more. I brought somebody to see you. This is Vangie Jamison. Edna Wolsky."

"Hello," Edna said. "Are you his girl friend?" I got a funny look from Vangie.

"*You're* my girl friend," I said. "I can't have two. It's not allowed in this state. So, Edna, this time tomorrow you'll have a nice new kidney. And you could stop with the machine."

"Will you be here when they put it in?" she said.

"They wouldn't let me in the operating room. But I'll be here afterward."

"Don't bring her," she said. "I just want you."

"Edna, is that nice? Somebody comes to visit you — "

"I don't have to be nice to everybody," she said. "I'm sick."

"It's all right, Edna," Vangie said. "I understand. I think you're nice, anyway."

"They stick you with knives," the child said. "I don't like it."

"You won't feel anything," Vangie said. "And you don't have to be afraid. You're not going to die."

"How do you know?"

"I'm sort of a witch," Vangie said. "I can see ahead some-

100

times. And I just saw you, in my head, you were back in this room, dressing a doll I'm going to send you. You wouldn't be able to do that if you were dead."

The child looked at her with her big, scared eyes. "What kind of a doll?"

"You'll see. You'll like her."

When we were ready to leave, a few minutes later, Edna held up her arms to Vangie too.

At the school I said, "I forgot about lunch. You still got time?"

"No. I'd like to but I'll be late for my class. I'll have a sandwich later."

"Don't forget," I said. "Don't run yourself down. Young people got the idea they could get away with everything, because they are young."

She started to go, and stopped. "You really took me in," she said. "You shouldn't fool people."

"I'm sorry, Vangie. I wanted to hear your ideas."

"You can hear them anytime. Without tricking me."

"All right, next time I'll just ask. Please excuse me."

"Okay. I'm glad you took me to see Edna, though. She's a lucky girl."

"Yes. Very lucky. A girl eleven years old, already her kidneys are shot. And the girl who got killed by a motorcycle, so there's a kidney her parents could sell for Edna — she's lucky too. What kind of a miserable world is this? Where is God? Ask the rabbi next time you see him. Maybe he'll tell you. Between the potato pancakes."

"What I get from Rabbi Strawse," she starts to say.

"Strawse?" I said. "What Strawse? His name is Strauss."

"Well, that's how he pronounces it."

"Already I know he's a faker," I said.

"He seems very sincere to me. What I get from him is

101

that we ought to concern ourselves more with what we can do for God, not what he has to do for us."

"I told you he's a faker," I said. "He copied it from Kennedy. He put in God instead of country. All right, go to your Spanish class. I don't want to make you late. *'Al que madruga, Dios le ayuda.'* "

"What does it mean? I'm not that far along."

"The early bird catches the worm. Something like it."

"How do you know that?"

"A taxi driver told me. In Córdoba."

"You're fabulous," she said.

"Thank you," I said. "I'll tell my analyst tomorrow. He thinks I'm retarded."

When she left, I thought about it and I came to the conclusion that Rabbi Strawse has got something, whoever he copied it from. A couple of times a year I say Kaddish for my father. Still, after thirty years. Rosh Hashanah and Yom Kippur. Don't ask me why. I stopped believing long ago. But next time when I'm telling God how great he is, and how merciful and how just, the only God, the God of Gods, the All Powerful — I'll try to remember to ask him, instead of what he could do for me, what I could do for him. Me, Seidman, an old *shnook*, like my father before me.

Yesterday I got a call from my sister Bessie; she decided to make a shower for Vangie to celebrate her engagement to Ralph. This is not exclusively a Jewish type occasion; it's a difference mainly between watercress sandwiches and chopped liver, but the general idea is the same as with the Gentiles: you bring a present for the bride-to-be and make sure the name of the store where you bought it is on the box so it could be exchanged.

Bessie needs an advice about a couple of things. First, I

102

should ask my *shicksa* daughter-in-law what is the right wording for the invitation. Miss Evangeline Jamison and Ralph Brandeis Immerman. This is the first time I heard that Ralph's middle name is Brandeis; what I remember is that it was Avrom after our grandfather on Mama's side. I told you how this kind of pretense turns me right away into a Rumpelstiltskin but I held myself back. I must really be getting old; lately the price for making this kind of a point with my sister seems too high.

She wants also for me to check the financial standing of the guest list she is making up. If Ralph is going to be a lawyer, what is the point of inviting a bunch of *shleppers* whose husbands make less than twenty-five thousand a year? If they got legal problems they go to the ACLU or to the small claims court where they could get them handled for free.

"What about some of Vangie's friends," I said. "Don't you think they should be invited?"

No, she didn't think so. Who could they be? Topless girls from her last job, or Mohammedans or Episcopalians they wouldn't fit in. "If she's going to be a member of this family," Bessie said, "she's got to get used to not bringing in a bunch of floozies and misfits."

"I still think you should consult her," I said.

"What's to consult? *I'm* giving the shower. She'll get an invitation, like everybody else."

And she hung up, to talk next to Sophie, about the menu.

In the afternoon, Vangie came in my office, she had on one of the new dresses in the line. "Harold wanted you to see this," she said. "I mean, Mr. Seidman Junior."

"If Mr. Seidman Junior wants from me an opinion about this dress," I said, "he's got to bring it in himself, on a hanger. On you everything looks good. We could have a big season in potato sacks, if you would cooperate."

"I should have you for breakfast instead of alfalfa sprouts," she said, but she didn't smile.

"You wouldn't like me for breakfast," I told her. "You could check this with my wife and daughter. I think now they are sorry they made me go to an analyst. Before I was depressed. Now I'm impossible."

She gives me now a polite smile and says, "Shall I tell Harold you like the dress?"

"Tell him I like it but I wouldn't commit myself until I see it on a hanger." She starts to go to the door and I said, "Don't go yet. Stay and talk to the old man a little."

She comes back and stands in front of my desk and looks at me for a minute. "Mr. Seidman, why did you turn over the business to Harold? I mean — you seem much too young to retire — or semi-retire, as you say."

"Vangie, I'm going to be fifty-six years old in a few months."

"You think that's old?"

"Don't you?"

"I guess I'm not age-conscious. When I was fourteen I had a big thing for my French teacher. He must have been sixty, at least. I never thought of him as old."

"You are not following the pattern. What I hear, fourteen-year-olds today think twenty-five is ancient."

"Oh, I think a lot of that is newspaper talk. Good copy. Anyway, you don't look fifty-six. More like forty-six. Going on forty."

"Thank you. You agree with my wife, she told me a few weeks ago, I was still a young, vigorous, exciting man. Then she turned off Cary Grant on the Late Show, gave me four vitamin E tablets and sent me to an analyst."

She laughed. Should go on a record, that laugh. Along with the great arias. "You're not going?" she said.

104

"To an analyst? Yes. You don't believe in it?"

"I don't know anything about it. It just wouldn't occur to me that you were a candidate for that sort of thing."

"Well, I'm giving it a trial. You asked me why I retired. I always figured to get out of this business while I was young enough to enjoy other things that I could afford now. But it didn't work out like I figured. Looks like you've got to have some purpose in life, Vangie, not just to amuse yourself. I haven't found it yet. I could go on making *shmatess* another ten, fifteen years, of course. But doesn't appeal to me."

"What's *shmatess?*"

"It's a pet name for dresses."

"Would it be all right if I called them *shmatess?*"

"In here, yes. With the customers, no. I think you better just say dresses."

"But what does it mean, actually? *Shmatess?*"

"Rags," I said.

"I see. Pejorative."

"Now *you* translate. What's pejorative?"

"Disparaging. Derogatory."

"Ah hah," I said. "Put down."

Now she really smiled. "Any time you decide to get rid of some of those *shmatess* in the showroom at the price of rags, I'd like a chance to bid."

"Vangie, you don't have to bid. You are practically family now, you could have whatever you want. It would be my pleasure. And Mr. Seidman Junior's too."

The smile got a little embarrassed. I could see she wanted to change the subject. "You said you had a daughter."

"Yes. About your age. A little older. Twenty-three."

"And she still lives at home."

"In a way. We've got a nine-room apartment, they made

105

them this way in the old days, and we remodeled it so Jenny's got three rooms to herself, with a separate entrance; sometimes when I want to get in touch with her I've got to send her a telegram. But lately, since I'm retired, or semi-retired, it wouldn't fit for me to come to the shop before ten, ten-thirty, so this is the time I use to keep up with the newspapers and periodicals, I subscribe to that French magazine, *Realités* and also, since I was not long ago in Spain, to *La Prensa*, the foreign edition, I don't get too much out of them but since I figure I'm not going to be invited to join the jet set, this is the next best thing to give myself a feeling I'm an international character. And as an extra dividend, I get to see my daughter sometimes at breakfast. I *see* her, mind you. Talking with her is another thing. She can't talk before she's had her coffee, and after she's had her coffee, we haven't found yet a subject on which she cares to hear my opinion. She's a Jewish princess, no use to try to hide it, Vangie. You read the article in the *New York* magazine maybe?

"Yes. I thought it was slanted."

"Maybe. But not unfriendly, actually. It's a phenomenon, no question. My Jenny is really a very nice girl. It's not her fault she thinks money is a convenience, like toilet tissue. I encouraged her to feel this way. I didn't know I was doing it but if it's anybody's fault, it's mine."

"What does your analyst say about that?"

"He says I've got a guilt complex. Actually, he doesn't say this, it's old-fashioned. He says I need to understand more about my eagerness to assume blame. I think he thinks I'm a *shmuck*, excuse the expression, and don't ask what it means, I couldn't explain it."

"I happen to know," she says. "A willing patsy. More or less."

106

"Yes. More or less. Tell me, Vangie, did you have a quarrel with Ralph lately?"

"No. Well, not exactly." She gave me now a real smile, lit up my whole office. (If you are sitting with a red pencil, to mark down all the corny expressions I use, I will change this one a little. Say it lit *me* up, my mood, fifty watts.) "Is your radar turned on?" she said.

"When you came in," I said, "you looked, I don't know, not so *yontevdik*."

"Those words," she said. "I'll bet you make some of them up."

"No," I said. "I speak nothing but the King's Yiddish. You could ask the rabbi." I was feeling actually a little frisky, for a change. She is such a refreshing person, somehow, it's such a pleasure just to look at her.

"What does it mean — *yontevdik?*" She made a new word out of it, the way she said it.

"It means the way a girl should look who's twenty-one — "

"Twenty-two. Last week."

"That's not nice, Vangie. You should have told me. All right, twenty-two, and beautiful, and in love, and going to be married — "

"Whoa," she said. "Let's take those one at a time. Beautiful. That's one of those all-purpose words — "

"I know. Could be an aria from *Tosca*, or spaghetti al pesto at San Marino, or a prizefighter who just gave his opponent such a *klop* in the mouth you wonder will he have any teeth left. Beautiful, man. And the opposite is not ugly, man. Stinks, man. Right?"

"Right. You've a good ear, Mr. Seidman."

"My daughter helps out. But you know what I mean when I say you are beautiful. Not like spaghetti al pesto."

"My looks are okay," she said. "As long as they last, I

won't have to settle for less than what pleases me in male companionship."

"Vangie, what kind of talk is that?"

"Plain talk. With someone I think well enough of, and feel close enough to, to talk plainly."

It was a nice gift and, for once, I wanted to keep it just like it was and not start a discussion with her about whether I deserved it.

"You want to do something for me, Vangie?" I said. "Say yes."

"Yes. But shouldn't I know what?"

"I want to make you a dress for your engagement party."

"What!"

"My sister is making an engagement party for you."

"Well, that's nice. This is the first I've heard of it. Did she indicate who I'm supposed to be getting engaged to?"

"Vangie — "

"You know, I'm sorry to say it but this woman's pretty close to being a freak. If I wanted to marry Ralph, which I don't, she'd have ruined it for us by now, single-handed."

"All right, calm down. You could concentrate on other members of the family."

She gives me a half smile. "Will you do something for me and head her off. Please?"

"You're sure? You don't want to think about it?"

"I'm sure. If I think about it, I might end up doing the woman a mischief."

"I got a pretty good idea what will happen, Vangie. If I tell her you don't want the party, she'll say you're just nervous about meeting a lot of new people and you'll get over it and I should butt out of it and everything will be fine."

"Well, please try. If I talk to her, it'll surely end up with me losing my temper and her crying and saying she should have known from the beginning that I was an anti-Semite."

108

We laughed, and I felt a little bit like a conspirator with her and I thought I should ask about Ralph.

"I don't think he's heard anything about this either," she said. "He hasn't mentioned it to me."

"You don't think he would want it?"

"I'm sure he wouldn't," she said. "But in any case, *I* don't want it."

"How is Ralph these days, Vangie?" I asked her.

"Okay," she said. "Back to his comfortable C minus average."

"Well, some people are late starters," I said. "Like Henry Ford."

"And Grandma Moses," she said. "I better get back to work or I'll get fired."

I got a call from Ralph. "Hi, Unk," he says, this is his name for me now, I suppose he fell into it naturally, it's short and sweet, like Pig. What he wants is for Unk to stop his mother from giving the shower.

"I got this request already from Vangie," I said. "What is going on with you two? You're going to get married, or not?"

"That's still up the flagpole," he says. "We're not going to be pressured into it, that's for sure. Anyhow, what's the point of Vangie meeting a bunch of five-pointed squares from the Hadassah whom she'll never see again? Who gets engaged nowadays, for Christ's sake?"

"It's true," I said. "Used to be the custom for pregnant girls. But now with the pill I suppose it's a foolish formality."

"Unk," he says, "I know you think our values are cockeyed. It's mutual and let's leave it at that, okay? Your generation abdicated — "

"Where are you?" I said.

"What?"

"Where are you calling from?"

"A phone booth. Why?"

"Tear out the phone so the company will know what you think of their principles. You got your little red book?"

"Unk," he says.

"Go read it to the squirrels in Central Park. For me, do me a big favor and forget my telephone number. I don't want any more calls from you. I heard enough of your bullshit for a lifetime."

I listened. There was only a little scripping noise on the wire, like a dying computer. Finally I heard Ralph's voice. "What'd you say, Unk?"

"I said I don't want to hear any more bullshit about my generation and how we abdicated. Okay?"

"Hey, Unk," he says. "We've got to get together sometime and really rap."

"Why? You think I'm a better prospect for your bullshit because I learned how to say the word?"

"It shows your mind isn't totally ossified. I mean closed. Look, Unk, about this marriage bit," he says, "I'd like you to understand. To me, when you — I don't mean just you, I mean all of you, my pop too — when you thought you were making such a great deal for yourselves by getting married, all you were doing was signing some papers and mouthing some gibberish so you could get laid regularly. With all the *yentehs* nodding approval, instead of banding together to run your cock out of the community before their husbands could get wind of what was going on. Let's face it, you sold your balls for a mess of Flatbush."

"I live on Central Park West. When did your parents live in Flatbush?"

"I'm using the word semantically. You know what I mean."

"Balls to you is also semantic? Listen, Mr. Ambassador from the Great People's Republic of China, I don't know about your father's balls but the last time I looked, the mortgage on mine was paid up. The title is free and clear. What about your balls? What's your intentions, once and for all, with Vangie?"

"Well, we're on a trial separation now — "

"The timing couldn't be better," I said. "Does your mother know?"

"My mother hasn't got time to listen. She's too busy making the shower."

"Whose idea is this trial separation? Yours or Vangie's?"

"Well, she suggested it and I agreed. Look, Vangie's a great chick — "

"If that means she is a wonderful, beautiful girl, and brilliant too, one in a million, I agree with you one hundred percent. And I congratulate you, you've got such an efficient, economical vocabulary."

"Come on, Unk. Just because I don't foam at the mouth. You know how I feel about Vangie. She really turns me on."

"I *don't* know how you feel about Vangie, really. Or how Vangie feels about you. I would like to know. I heard something about E above high C but is this the whole story?"

"E above high C? I don't get it."

"Why do you need a separation now?"

"Well, we both want to think about our situation, without it being all clouded up by sex. Vangie's really freaked out on this archaeology bit and I don't know how that'd work out for us. She's been having second thoughts too. Like I told you, it was her suggestion that we rear back and take a long, cool look at our relationship."

Well, maybe this is really intelligent, what they're doing.

I don't like what Ralph said, it's typical of the young people, they think to be honest, or what they think is honest, they've got to talk like bums. But when I look back, I've got to admit there's something to it. Wasn't such a terrific success, the old-style marriages when before you knew what was what, there was a child on the way and your life as an individual was over. You were a husband and a parent, and finished with everything else.

Could they be right, the kids? All the star gazing, the sentiment, the love poetry, only a trick so people should be tied together and have children, and for the rest, who cares if they've got to stumble through life afterward, any which way, hooked up like in a three-legged race?

"What would you like to talk about today?" Dr. Vogel asked me. I started to laugh and he said, "What amuses you?"

"I was going to say 'what would *you* like to talk about?' and then I thought of a funny scene from a movie called *Marty*, this *shlemiel* and his friend have got nothing to do, nowhere to go and they spend five minutes like this, saying to each other 'what would you like to do, Marty' — 'I don't know, what would *you* like to do?' It was funny, and the same time it was sad too."

"You feel sad this morning?"

"No. Not more than usual. I ought to feel glad. My son showed me the report on the last six months' operations, the dress business is lousy now, we were expecting to show a loss and there's a profit."

"But it didn't raise your spirits."

"No. I wish I could say yes. But didn't mean a thing."

"You think it's possible that there may be some resentment mixed into your feeling about your son's success in handling the business?"

"Don't be foolish, doctor. This crazy I'm not. I'm proud of him. Maybe if he was a candidate for a Nobel prize in medicine, or literature, I would be more proud. I mean, the achievement. But about the boy himself, I never had any reason to feel anything but proud of him. This we don't have to spend time on, doctor. You could take my word for it, Oedipus shmoedipus."

"I believe you, Mr. Seidman. Tell me about your business. When did you start it?"

"You mean my son's business."

"It still goes by the name of Seidman and Son, doesn't it?"

"Yes."

"An important name in the garment industry, I'm told. Why are you so intent on dissassociating yourself from it?"

"Because it sucked the life out of me for thirty years and it's enough. I don't want any strings hanging from me I should get tied back every time there is a crisis."

"But from what you've told me there seems no need to anticipate any crises."

"Doctor, you heard the expression, if you're over fifty and you wake up in the morning and nothing hurts, don't congratulate yourself, you're dead? Well, in the dress business, if you open up your shop in the morning and there's no crisis waiting, you could call in the creditors, you got no more business."

He doesn't laugh. He squeezed out a little smile. What it would take to get a real laugh from this man I don't know. And what I don't know, more, is why I should keep trying to make him laugh. On my money. It's kind of stupid, the whole thing.

"You started the firm yourself?" he says now.

"You mean did somebody give me a push?"

"I mean you didn't take it over from someone else."

"What I took over was an empty loft on Bleecker Street,

with four secondhand Singer sewing machines, one broken."

"In other words you started with nothing."

"Don't say nothing. I had two hundred dollars cash and a line of credit from the delicatessen store on the corner."

"And you built up a million dollar business."

"Two million eight last year."

"Starting during the depression, against tough competition, surviving the depression — "

"And two hundred and eighteen visits from the union delegate."

"To me this seems a considerable achievement. Why do you feel a need to disparage it?"

"Because like I told you, I've been around a little, I've seen things, the Sistine Chapel and the Rodin Museum, and I've heard a few things, like *Don Giovanni,* and I read a few things, like *War and Peace,* and lately about a man named Stephens who discovered the ruins of Palenque — and to spend thirty years building a dress business seems to me now a rotten waste of a lifetime, if you want the truth."

"You've some years ahead of you. Have you thought of starting something else?"

"You mean with a twenty-two-year-old girl?" I don't know why I said it. It just came out and right away I was sorry.

"You'll have to explain that," he says.

"Never mind. Forget I said it. What else am I going to start? Playing the violin? Painting flowers? Go digging in Yucatán for another Palenque?"

"You're interested in archaeology?"

"Yes. It's a fascinating subject."

"Has it always been one of your interests?"

"No, I just started to read up on it lately." I realized suddenly where he's going. He doesn't get his money for nothing, this man. He knows his business, believe me. "You

114

told me," he said, "that there's a model in your place who's interested in archaeology."

"When did I tell you this?"

"In our very first session."

"You listen good, doctor. It's not true, like they show in the movies that psychiatrists are always taking naps while their patients are on the couch, talking."

"What about this model?"

"Nothing. I told you she's a beautiful girl, she's interested in archaeology, she works in the place three mornings a week and two afternoons so she could continue her school."

"You also told me she's sleeping with your nephew."

"That's right. They're supposed to get married."

"Supposed?"

"Yes, supposed. You know, you could drive a person crazy, doctor. Every word has got to be examined for defects six times before it passes inspection."

"I've told you, Mr. Seidman, words are the only things we have to work with here. And they can serve a double purpose. They can reveal or they can disguise."

"What have I got to disguise? My sister gave me a commission, in the first place, I should break up this affair between my nephew and the girl, she thought they were going to get married and she was ready to commit suicide."

"Why?"

"She was sure the girl was a bum, working in a topless joint, she's a Gentile besides; well, turns out she's a jewel, and now my sister is ready to commit suicide if they *don't* get married."

"Is there any reason they shouldn't?"

"No reason, except the girl doesn't want to. But this is not relevant, my sister would say, if she knows the word. You told me you think I enjoy feeling depressed, well this woman is only happy when she's living in a state of complete *toomel* —"

"Translate that for me."

"I don't know — confusion, agitation, always a crisis — I don't worry too much when she tells me she's going to commit suicide because the worst she would do is throw herself out of a ground-floor window so she could maybe sprain a wrist or get a little water on the knee, and everybody would have to come to the hospital and bribe the nurses not to quit. This woman could maybe use some analysis but I wouldn't be doing you a favor if I sent her to you as a patient."

"Let's get back to the girl. Vangie?"

"Yes. Evangeline Jamison. Her parents live in Canada, Montreal. She's got a very interesting background."

"You approve of her relationship with your nephew?"

"What's to approve? Who asked me for my approval?"

"*I'm* asking you if you approve. What do you think of the arrangement?"

"You mean that she's sleeping with him, before they are married? I don't know what to tell you. I grew up with different ideas but who knows if they were better ideas. You could say better than I. I'm sure you see in your office plenty of times the results of marriage the way we figured it should be. All I could tell you is this is a fine, decent girl, I never met in my life anyone more straight and honest, and I got to assume that what she is doing is straight and honest too. For her, the way she wants to live."

"How do you feel about your nephew?"

"I don't know. I've got mixed feelings now. He's a big, handsome boy, but a *draykopf*, in my estimation — "

"What does that mean?"

"I don't know how to translate it. Scatterbrain maybe, but this is not fair to Ralphie, just to say this; in some ways

116

he is a brilliant boy and anyway if Vangie picked him out to have a relationship with, I've got to think there's something to him, more than I gave him credit for."

"And you think they should get married."

"Doesn't matter what I think. It's what she thinks — or what they both think."

"It matters here what *you* think. What *do* you think?"

"Well, if I had the right to tell Vangie what to do, I think I would give her the money to stop working, go to school full time, get her degree and then go dig in Yucatán."

"What stops you from making the offer?"

"What stops you from running in front of a bus? I'm depressed, not crazy. Or am I?"

"You're afraid of what people would say."

"Yes. People named Sophie, Jenny, Harold, Bessie — "

"Your family. Do you think they have the right to smother your impulses?"

"What do you think, doctor?"

"Mr. Seidman, I've said it before, and I'll say it again, and as many times as I have to until it sinks in: I'm not here to make judgments. My function is to help you find out what you actually think and feel, what you really want."

"Suppose I would find out that what I really want is to commit suicide."

"I don't think we need concern ourselves about that. You're not psychotic."

"There's more than one way to commit suicide."

"You mean, figuratively."

"Wouldn't be figurative if my wife divorced me, my daughter disowned me, I became an outcast in my family and a dirty old man for everybody else."

"All that because you made a generous gesture — "

"Who would believe it's only a generous gesture? My sister, Bessie, for instance? Or Ralphie? I'm getting already sideways looks in the shop because I'm interested in this girl and her future and we go for coffee sometimes and talk."

"Is her future all you're interested in, Mr. Seidman?"

"You see what I mean? I'm getting the sideways look from you too."

"Take my word for it, I'm looking straight at you, not sideways. I've no interest in your motives other than to make them clear to you."

"How could you stay so aloof, doctor. Don't you have *some* feeling for your patients? What they are going through."

"Of course. But I have to keep them strictly in check. The moment I let my feelings intrude — sympathy, pity, anger, disgust, whatever — my usefulness as an analyst is at an end."

"Listen," I said. "Let's stop. I've got a terrific headache."

"All right. The hour's about up anyway. I'll see you again on Friday."

III

I had a funny thing in the shop today. I don't mean humorous. Left me feeling a little upset. First of all, I went in the showroom and Vangie was alone there, in a bra and panties, holding a dress. I turned away and she said, "Don't do that. You've seen me before."

"It's a reflex," I said. I turned back and watched her put on the dress. She's got the kind of figure that even on a sour morning could remind you you've still got a nodding acquaintance with sex. She fixed herself in the mirror and came over and said, "I think this dress is smashing — " She stopped and gave me a look. "Hey," she said, "you don't look so *yontevdik* today."

"I've got a reason," I said. "I found out I've got an incurable disease."

Her face got real pale and I said, quick, "It's incurable but not serious. I'm suffering from old age."

The color started to come back to her face. "That's a lousy joke," she said.

"I know. I'm sorry." And then I did something foolish, I guess, it was so touching to me she should give a damn, I took her hand and put it to my lips. This is not exactly natural to my character and training on Seventh Avenue, to kiss somebody's hand like an old boulevardier; it was kind of odd actually, I don't know what made me do it and, naturally, that minute, Harold came in, said "oops" like he would have stumbled into a porno movie. Then he says, "Sorry," and starts out.

"What are you sorry about?" I said.

"I thought I might be interrupting something."

"Don't be a jackass," I said. "You want something?"

"I'd like Miss Jamison to show that dress to the designer." And he goes out.

"I'd better show her the dress," Vangie said.

"She could wait. I'm still the Chairman of the Board."

"You don't seem very happy about it."

"I'm upset today. I mean, more than usual."

"You want to tell me about it?"

"I saw a movie, couple of years ago, maybe you saw it, I can't remember the title, there was a warden of a chain gang, a big brute of a man, he's holding a piece of wood or a rubber hose or something and he's slapping it real gentle against the palm of his other hand, and he says to a prisoner who's always giving him trouble, 'What we got here is a little problem in communication.' Well, what I got is a little problem in communication with my daughter, only what I haven't got is a rubber hose I could use to open up the lines."

She was smiling now but in back of the smile I could see she's got sympathy for what I'm saying. I thought, why could I communicate so easy with this girl and not my own daughter?

"What's the problem?" she said.

"The problem is she's keeping company now — what's the matter?"

"No," she said. "You didn't say it."

"What?"

"Keeping company."

"Something's wrong with it?"

"No. Nothing's wrong with Tiffany glass and Currier and Ives either."

"I don't understand you, Vangie."

"I'm sorry. I just never thought I'd hear anything like that aloud in my time."

"You mean you just found out I'm old-fashioned."

"I just found out on you it's beautiful. Tell me about your daughter. She's keeping company, you said."

"You're laughing at me."

"You know better than that. I'm adoring you. Come on."

"Well, this new boy friend — why should I call him boy friend, he's not a boy and he's not her friend, he's maybe thirty-eight and he's married and where could such a relationship go? He's somebody in TV, a vice president in charge of programming with one of the big networks, so I said to her last night, she came flying in to ask her mother for a scarf or something and I said to her, 'You're going out with Mr. CBS this evening?' 'Yes,' she says, 'he's picking me up in a few minutes.' 'He wouldn't have time, I suppose, to give a hello to your mother and father, say something about the weather?' This is a legitimate question, no?"

"Go on," Vangie says.

" 'Come on, pa,' Jenny says, like she's talking to a backward child, 'we've got a reservation at Caravelle for nine o'clock.' 'Could you give me an idea of your intentions with this Armenian Casanova?' I said and she turns to me, real fresh and says, 'My intentions are to have dinner with him which should take us until about ten-thirty and what my intentions are after that are none of your business.' "

"Well," Vangie says, "that's a great start toward total communication."

"You think what I said was wrong?"

"You want an honest answer?"

"I don't think you are capable of anything else."

"Oh yes, I am," she says. "I'm not a revolutionary, like Ralph. I don't burn with a pure red flame. I don't want to carry that banner with the strange device through snow and ice and freeze my ass off. I'd lie a little if it suited my purpose, and didn't hurt anybody. But if you want my honest answer now, yes, I think you were wrong. You said your daughter's twenty-three. That's old enough by a couple of years, legally, so she's got a right — outside of the rights guaranteed her by the Constitution — to make her own decisions about what she does."

"And I've got a right to pay her bills and watch her make a mishmash of her life and shut up."

"You've got a right, if you want to use it, to be furious and critical and disapproving, but if you do you're passing up the chance of having any meaningful dialogue with her. Okay, I've used the vomitous phrase. Now *I'll* shut up."

"I guess you think I'm an old fogy too, like Jenny."

"I don't know what Jenny thinks but you'd be amazed at what I think."

"Tell me. Amaze me."

"I think you're a turn-on."

"What is that? A jokester?"

"No."

"Then what?"

"I don't think I'll tell you. You're having too good a time these days, putting yourself down. I don't want to spoil your fun."

"Vangie, to feel depressed all the time, old, useless — you think I'm having fun with this?"

"You must. You seem to keep working at it."

"You could be my psychoanalyst," I said.

"No, I couldn't. But we could spend an evening together sometime and talk. I listen good when I'm interested." She stopped for a minute, then she said, "I'm free tonight."

"You haven't got a date with Ralph?"

"Obviously. Did you think I meant a threesome?"

"Don't make me sound like an idiot, Vangie. Isn't it natural I should ask about Ralph?"

"No. Not when I've just suggested that we spend an evening together. You feel obliged to monitor my relationship with Ralph?"

"Monitor is not the same as being concerned, Vangie. You are very touchy this morning. Reminds me of home."

"I'm sorry." She gave me a kind of smile now. "You don't need two Jennys in your life, do you? What about my offer?"

I didn't answer right away and she said, "You have to check in at home, I suppose."

"Not necessarily," I said. "I could tell my wife I'm going to spend this evening with Ralphie's girl and spend the next two weeks explaining her why. Or I could just stay out and wait for her to call the Missing Persons Bureau."

"That's great," she said. "Everywhere I look I see these great advertisements for marriage."

"Vangie, I made a joke. My wife doesn't keep a time clock in the hall where I got to punch in. She's a loving and understanding woman and lately she's got a lot to put up with, with my moods. Besides, you shouldn't make any conclusions about marriage from me. My idea of being married was doing things together. Not only in bed. Just happens I never found anybody who is better company than my wife. I'm not a bowler, or a card player, lodge meetings are for me a bore, I would rather just be at home with her. If we don't go to the theater, or a concert, or a movie. I read somewhere a very nice line: 'He needed solitude, the way some plants need shade.' Well, I could understand very well that there's certain temperaments like this. Artists, I suppose. Creative people. But with me it's exactly the opposite. I hate being alone. Sophie and I could be at home and I'm reading, or listening to the record player, and maybe we don't exchange a dozen words the whole evening, but there's the feeling we're together and I couldn't overestimate to you the value of this feeling.

"Well, if you set a pattern like this for more than thirty years, you can't change it suddenly and expect the other person is not going to be confused. It's not marriage that's responsible. This is the way I wanted it."

"Okay," she said. *"De gustibus non est disputandum.* That's what's left of three years of Latin."

"What does it mean?"

"Every man to his own poison. I'd better go show this dress to the designer before she comes unglued."

She walked away to the designing room. I knew I got her upset too, but I couldn't tell you why.

I told Dr. Vogel about this conversation.

"What does this girl mean to you?" he said.

"What do you mean, what does she mean to me? She is Venus Rising from the Foam."

"Are you going to see her?"

"I see her every day in the shop."

"Are you going to see her alone?"

"You think I should?"

Silence.

"I was thinking about maybe spending an evening with her," I said. "She invited me. What is your opinion, should I do it?"

He doesn't say anything.

"For Christ's sake," I said, "what kind of a doctor are you, a person could be dying you wouldn't give him an opinion about anything?"

"You don't want an opinion from me, Seidman. You want my blessing."

"For what, for God's sake? To go talk to a girl who shows

124

a little interest? Who could give me a clue to what's going on in the world, what's going on in my own daughter's head?" I jumped up. "You know what I actually want from you, doctor? I want a final bill. I got enough of this crap."

I went to the door and he said, "You've got forty minutes left of your hour."

"For what?" I said. "More crap?"

"That's an uncommon word for you, Seidman. Is that the message Venus brought you, rising from the foam?"

I couldn't help myself, I laughed. He laughed a little too and said, "All right. Come back, relax and let's try to find out what this girl really means to you."

I did something peculiar today. I lied to Sophie. The first time in our marriage. I told her I was having dinner with Larry. I didn't realize till later this would mean I'd have to call in Larry and tell him that if anybody asked, he should say we had dinner together that evening. He gave me a certain kind of a look, it was worse than a slap in the face from my father.

"So you've joined the club, Morris. Finally. You want the key to my apartment?"

"Thank you," I said. "Some other time. When I could bring my own records."

Vangie made me potato pancakes, very good, even if I burned myself a little swallowing them too fast. We talked about love. How did it start? I was still upset about Jenny and I asked her did she think it was unnatural for a girl, twenty-three, still living with her parents, to refrain from sex until she was married. "This is not possible in the modern world, Vangie?"

"Sure it's possible," she said. "Parents can warp their children so they end up with all kinds of problems."

"Warp?"

"Yes, warp. What does she do — I mean, you told me she still lives at home — "

"It's really separate. I told you, it's like her own apartment, she's got one room fixed up like a studio. She's interested in ceramics, she makes some very nice things. She even sold a couple. Wouldn't pay the rent, you understand — "

"Well, she sounds okay."

"I didn't say anything else, Vangie. She's a fine, intelligent girl — "

"And knowing you, I'd bet she doesn't have any hang-ups about sex."

"You mean it's only me that's got the hang-ups."

"I mean that if she's going with a man who turns her on, they just naturally ball."

"Ball?"

"They go to bed. You asked me what I think. That's what I think."

It's what I've been thinking myself, but hearing her say it made me feel a little sick. Doesn't do any good to try to rationalize, I can't get used to the idea. I saw Jenny somehow different. Maybe it's just that I'm jealous. I read enough psychology to know you have to think about this, with a father and daughter. Seems to me a fantastic idea but for me, lately, the whole world is a Luna Park.

Vangie must have noticed something in my expression because she said, "Look, this talk is upsetting you. Let's stop. How about some brandy."

"Thanks, no, but I'll have some more coffee if you've got it."

"I'll make a fresh pot," she said.

"Doesn't have to be perked," I told her. "Could be instant."

"That's a dirty word," she said. "Instant. Frozen. Preservatized. Additived, dehydrated, decaffeinized, hydrogenated — what I'd like is a well and a bucket, nearby, where I could go and draw my own water — "

"You want to throw away all the modern conveniences. Cook on a wood stove, I suppose. Catch a fresh fish for breakfast in the East River — "

"Let's drop the subject," she said. "Ridicule's the easiest, and cheapest way to hang onto prejudices. If you're not concerned about being processed to death, good luck. Here, take a look at the ninth wonder of the world."

She dumps in my lap a big book with pictures of the Anthropological Museum in Mexico City. I got lost a little, turning the pages. After a while she came back with the coffee and gave me a cup.

"How about that," she said, pointing to the book.

"Magnificent," I said.

"That's only a tiny part of the collection. And the building itself — have you ever been to Mexico?"

"No."

"You ought to go. Just that museum is worth the trip."

"We talked about it, my wife and I. She's afraid of the food. We heard stories. The way they grow things down there — the fertilizer and so on — it's a little too natural."

I didn't want to antagonize her but, after all, I don't have to be intimidated either by a twenty-two-year-old girl. She gave me a look but I could see she wasn't really angry.

"Vangie," I said, "excuse me for making fun. You know how much respect I've got for your opinions. I know you think about things, I know you don't pick up ideas just to have something to hit us older people on the head with. It would be a tragedy for me now if you would stop 'communicating' because I couldn't agree with everything you say, the first minute you say it. After all, takes a little time to adjust."

"Okay," she said. "How's the coffee?"

127

"Delicious. Tell me, Vangie, what did you mean when you said to me the other day that I was a turn-on."

"Forget it," she said. "I was just *hocking a tchynik.*"

"Amazing, what a gift you've got for languages. Tell me what you meant."

"No."

"Why?"

"I know you. It'll only embarrass you."

"Suddenly you're worried about embarrassing me? Come on, Vangie."

"Okay. Fasten your seat belt. It's what the kids say about a man who makes them think about going to bed."

"And getting a good night's sleep," I said, quick. I could feel myself getting red in the face. I didn't want her to see I really *was* embarrassed, so I took a gulp of the coffee and I said, like this would be a philosophy discussion — I must have sounded like a real *shnook* — "Everything is sex today, with the kids. Anyway, from what I see in the movies. One, two, three, into bed; afterward it maybe occurs to them to ask, 'by the way, what's your name?' This man who comes to see my Jenny, you would think maybe sometimes he would stay long enough to have a drink, or a cup of coffee, find out if we are Democrats or Republicans, say hello and good-bye — what happened to courting, to manners, to love, Vangie? What's going on in the world that makes me feel I don't belong in it anymore?"

The look she gave me now, I could only call it tender. But maybe it was pity. "You really want to talk about love?" she said.

"Yes. Why do you keep saying you don't know what it means?"

"Oh man," she said. "Here goes the ball game."

"You mean the balling game."

She laughed now, like she would have heard a child say something that tickled her. "That's a neat pun. Okay, love. When I was a kid, I mean nine or ten, there were two Bibles in our house. One was my grandmother's. If I had to mumble through Corinthians — you know what I'm talking about?"

"Yes. That *noodnick*, Paul. Letter to the Corinthians."

"Is the New Testament part of religious instructions for Jews?"

"Bite your tongue. Better a good Jew should read *Fanny Hill*. But I told you, I stopped being a good Jew when I was nine years old."

"Well, in my grandmother's Bible there was the passage: 'If I speak with the tongues of angels and have not charity, I am become as sounding brass, etcetera.' You know it?"

"Yes. He started out being a Jew, after all. He said a few good things."

"But in our regular Bible, the same passage read, 'If I speak with the tongues of angels and have not *love*.' So, first confusion. Is love charity, or charity love, or what? Okay, now I have to tell you about the chickens we had in our yard when I was a child. One of my mother's less kooky notions was that fresh eggs, snatched from the nest still warm, and eaten practically raw and slimy, were great for strengthening the bones of a growing girl. They were great for keeping me nauseated most of the time too. My mother hadn't heard of cholesterol, apparently, and she may have set me up for arteriosclerosis at an early age. But my bones are fine. They withstood several years of hockey in high school in Montreal, and those kids played rough.

"Anyway, there was a rooster, naturally, and what I felt for that bird was one of the purest emotions I've ever experienced. Pure hate. First off, his idea of dawn was four o'clock in the morning. And he didn't crow. He brayed. And he always kept at it until he saw the light go on in my room and knew that he'd got me up and out of bed. Then his behavior toward the hens always put me in a rage. He'd single one out, chase her, squawking and terrified, across the yard and when he'd run her down he'd jump on and maltreat her and then let her go, dazed and humiliated and miserable.

"I exploded to my mother one day about this constant outrageous bullying and she explained to me that what the rooster was doing was not bullying the hens and making their lives miserable. He was making love, she said. The first boy at school who wanted to make love got my knee in his crotch and I went through high school suspected of being a dyke."

"Excuse me, what is a dyke?" I said. "The only ones I know about are in Holland."

"There are a few in this country too. They turn up in outfits like Women's Lib and such."

"Ah ha. A dyke is someone who wants equal pay with men."

"Yes. And equal opportunity to court the same women. You're putting me on."

"Excuse me. I couldn't resist. I guess I'm a *badchen* at heart."

"What's that?"

"A clown."

"All right, I'll forgive you. By the way, this *noodnick,* Paul, as you call him — what is a *noodnick,* in your darling lexicon?"

"Well, he is somebody, if you say to him 'how are you' you are stuck for three hours getting an answer."

Again the laugh. "Marvelous language. Well, Paul says

somewhere, that it's better to marry than to burn, which to my mind is a bigger put-down of marriage than anything Betty Friedan ever thought of."

"Go on," I said. "Please. You were talking about love."

"Okay. Remember, you asked for this. Love is a four-letter word. Fuck has the same number of letters. Why does love bring teary smiles to the faces of the righteous, while fuck sends them screaming for the vice squad? Isn't that what's supposed to go on, not just with the kids, but among married people occasionally? Let's turn off the light and — shshsh, mustn't say the dirty word. And mustn't leave the light on because if you do, you'll likely see something kind of nasty going on.

"What *is* going on, actually? An exchange of charities? Is love really being made? Or hate? Or revenge? Or reproduction? Or habit? If you're supposed to love your neighbor, just how far do you go before it becomes fornication? Who's got the thesaurus? If I'm supposed to love my boy friend and my new dress and my Maker and fried chicken and my mother and father — father! Hell, man, isn't that what they call incest?"

"All right, Vangie," I said. "Maybe we better stop now." I felt actually a little dizzy. I tried to give her a smile.

"You're on the ropes, huh?" she said. "How about some more coffee."

"I might as well," I said. "I don't think I'll get much sleep tonight anyway."

"How do you feel today?" Dr. Vogel asked me.

"The same as last time, thank you. Rotten."

"What does rotten mean, Mr. Seidman."

"You never felt rotten in your life?"

"I've felt discouraged, overworked, underpaid, frustrated

131

— any or all of these could be described as feeling rotten."

"You really have such feelings, doctor? I thought you analysts were supposed to be immune."

"Nobody's immune, Mr. Seidman. We're learning that even animals experience these feelings."

I got a funny recollection from long ago, the time Harold got hurt and was in a hospital in Seoul — you know we still got soldiers over there who are being maimed and killed in "border clashes" they call them, you can find the items sometimes on page 38 in the newspapers; the soldiers are there, I suppose, to keep an eye on those North Koreans so if they send their navy to attack San Francisco we'll know about it in time. Anyway, we didn't hear from Harold for quite a while, and we were upset naturally, but with his dog, Hercules, it was like he knew something; he would lie around shivering, not eating, the expression on his face you could only describe it as worried sick. Maybe it was just my imagination but this is what I thought at the time, and what Dr. Vogel said just now reminded me of it.

"Let me straighten out a misconception you appear to have about analysis," I heard him say now. "Or rather about those of us who practice analysis. Have you ever heard something like this: 'This man calls himself a psychoanalyst? With a wife who drinks like that?' Or 'with those crazy children?' "

"Sounds familiar," I said. "Maybe I said something like it myself."

"Analysis isn't a miracle drug, Mr. Seidman, to make all of life's problems disappear. Either for our patients or ourselves. Many of us who have taken up the practice of analysis, were drawn to it in the first place because we were deeply troubled or disturbed. Part of our training involves a period of deep analysis and we continue to go back for more,

132

from time to time, even after we've been in practice for years. We're not immune, believe me, and we can't immunize our patients against the dangers and distortions and distresses of living. We have theories about character formation but actually we don't understand too much about it, and we don't feel we can do much to change character once it's been formed. All we can provide is some insight which helps people to cope with their problems. To see them in proper perspective. Change their attitudes. Psychoanalysis is not a science. There *are* a few things we do know, with a fair degree of certainty. We know, for instance, that depression is often the result — the by-product, or side effect — of concealed rage."

"All right. So what am I in a rage about?"

"Assuming I knew, it wouldn't do you a particle of good for me to tell you. You wouldn't accept it, you'd find endless reasons to refute me and we'd be exactly nowhere. You have to come to these realizations yourself. This technique we use, of turning questions back to the patient, for his own interpretations and conclusions, wasn't designed merely to annoy him. Surely you're intelligent enough to see that. Now you've told me you feel rotten. Can you be more specific? Do you have any idea what's making you feel rotten?"

"I think it's mostly because I don't feel anything. I told you before. I got the feeling the whole thing is a fake and I'm not interested anymore."

"You're bored? Is that it?"

"More than bored. Disgusted."

"Then you *are* interested. To the degree at least of experiencing disgust."

"I could see why it takes five years to get a diploma in analysis. You are worse than the Talmudists."

"Words are the only things we have to work with. Meaning is what we're after. Personal meaning for you. That's the only way to achieve insight. It's a tedious process, I admit. It's not wonderfully stimulating for me either. Gets pretty boring sometimes, I don't mind telling you. I'm fagged out after a day of it. But it's the only effective method I know of doing my work. It's easy for you to say 'rotten' or 'disgusted' and luxuriate in the feeling without having to grub for the real meaning, or feeling, behind those words. But I can't let you do that."

"That's kind of a funny word you used, doctor. Luxuriate. You mean I *enjoy* feeling rotten?"

"In a sense, yes. You're a logical man. If you had a headache you would take some aspirin — "

"Bufferin. It's twice as effective and doesn't upset your stomach. Don't you watch television, doctor?"

"Don't put me off. Are you afraid of gaining some insight?"

"Excuse me. I got this bad habit to make jokes — "

"It's not a bad habit, per se. Jokes have a value — sometimes they're designed to make the unbearable bearable. That's a special quality of Jewish humor; there's actually a kind of gallantry in it — why do you smile?"

"I was thinking about my father when he used to say *'a klug tzu Columbus.'* "

"A curse on Columbus?"

"Yes."

"For discovering America, presumably."

"Yes. So my father could discover it afterward, to his sorrow. Was this gallantry, this humor? I think he was just so tired of fighting to make a living, he didn't want anymore. He just gave up."

"You want to follow his example."

"It's not the same story with me — but maybe."

134

"I don't think so. I don't think you're here because your wife sent you. I think you want to fight the idea of giving up. And at the same time you're fighting my trying to help you. It's a paradox inherent in your situation. You're a proud man, you're not used to the idea of asking to be helped, not man or God either, I gather. You resent your having to come to me as a supplicant, so to speak, with me as the giver of aid, and you keep making these jokes to disguise your real feelings. And doing this you defeat your purpose in coming here. Why don't you let yourself believe that I know my business, that you need my help, that I want to help you, and *can* help you if you'll cooperate."

"All right. I want your help. I believe you know your business. What's next?"

"I'd like you to come to grips with something you said before."

"For instance."

"You said, didn't you, that there's nothing in your day-to-day living — nothing visible that is — to make you feel rotten."

"I said that?"

"Yes. Don't you remember?"

"Yes. Something like it. I'm glad you remember. Shows me you weren't *dremmling*, the first few sessions."

"Day dreaming?"

"Yes. Only you could *dremmle* at night too. Without sleeping. I couldn't tell, you kept sitting there with your eyes half closed, like a Buddha — "

"You'd have felt better if you got me angry, wouldn't you? If I'd lashed out at you — would that make you feel you'd gotten your money's worth?"

"Don't ask me riddles, doctor. I'm confused enough already."

135

"Is that what your father used to do?"

"Ha. You've got the right one. My father wouldn't lash out at a cockroach. But tell me, doctor, why *don't* you yell a little sometimes, tell me I'm a jerk — "

"Because that's a luxury I gave up when I decided to become a psychoanalyst. Now let's get back to your actual situation. You've got no financial worries, you told me, your children are — or should be from what you've said — a source of satisfaction to you. You don't have a nagging or unfaithful wife — "

"Wait a minute. Unfaithful. How do I know this? I don't keep tabs on her."

"You think it's a possibility?"

"Anything is a possibility. There's this fellow, Bernstein, a regular jet setter, an adjusted personality as you know, you gave him his diploma, collects for the UJA and drives a Mercedes 280 SE, and if you tell him there's lots of other cars he could buy, not from a company that's full of Nazis and Jew haters, he tells you it's time we closed the book on the past, and stopped hating, and Israel has been trading with Germany for fifteen years. Wouldn't surprise me if some day he comes up with an idea that it would be good for Israel to have an Egyptian prime minister. But my wife thinks he is very cute. You know what that means, cute?"

"Attractive?"

"More than attractive. Cute. You should see the face my daughter Jenny makes when she hears her mother use words like that. I could feel the whole generation gap opening up in the rug, right at my feet."

"You think your wife is capable of having an affair with Dr. Bernstein?"

"Why do you call him doctor? The man is a Ph.D. in some cockamamie subject like business administration. This

136

entitles him to be called doctor? You're a doctor. You think it's the same thing?"

"All right, let's call him Mr. Bernstein. Do you think your wife could have an affair with him?"

"Could have, I suppose yes. If she would do it, I don't know."

"Does it worry you?"

"Are you crazy? If you wouldn't have brought it up, the idea would never even enter my mind. Doesn't stop me from despising Mr. Bernstein though."

"You don't think he's cute."

"I think he is an idiot. And a faker. And what I despise most in the world is a faker."

"All right. You used the word 'disgusted' before. What was in your mind?"

"What was in my mind. Did you listen to the radio this morning?"

"Yes."

"Did you hear that in Vietnam yesterday we had a big *glick?*"

"Good fortune?"

"*What* a good fortune. Our planes killed sixty-four North Vietnamese in one bunch. Even if it's a lie and it was only thirty-four, or fourteen, this is some good news, no? Somebody going around counting dead bodies to make you a present of the list."

"You don't think we should be in Vietnam?"

"I don't think we should be killing. In Vietnam, or any place. But there is a big confusion in my mind about this too. My Harold, Jenny, my nephew Ralphie — they've got no problems how they feel. It's all very clear to them. They can afford to be cynical about this country and our system and our politics. I can't. I got in this country an oppor-

137

tunity for a kind of life I couldn't have dreamed of anywhere else in the world. Not only me. Millions like me.
The Communists say they want to destroy us. Capitalism.
Imperialism. What is capitalism? A building on Wall
Street? It's me. My neighbors. My lodge members. My
way of life. Your way of life. Maybe it's just noise they are
making, about destroying us. But maybe it's true. We didn't
believe *Mein Kampf* either, in the beginning. Maybe,
sooner or later, some place, some where, we will have the
final destruction they keep promising us. So maybe Vietnam
was the best place for us to send our soldiers to fight.

"But you come to a conclusion like this, you're afraid to
go look in a mirror, you'll see there some kind of a monster that makes the Werewolf of Paris look pretty by comparison. How could a sane person, supposed to have feelings,
compassion, ever say *this* is a good place, the best place, to
send a young man to die? Or to have his legs torn off. Or his
face shot away. Isn't this something to destroy your mind,
your reason, thinking about it? What kind of a world is it,
where thirteen-, fourteen-year-old boys are trained to be
terrorists, murderers? And in return we fry them like potato chips with napalm, all the time talking about peace
and freedom. Honoring treaties. God knows what. This is
not a world. It's a slaughterhouse. A lunatic asylum."

"Could it be, Mr. Seidman, that part of your feeling rotten is a sense of guilt because you're not doing anything
about it?"

"Like what? Go around getting signatures on a petition
to God to tell him to take a look and see what's going on?
Grow a beard and walk around with a placard? To say what?
That the world is crazy? Maybe you misunderstand me, doctor. I think the craziest of all are the Communists. And the
cruelest. They've got a program for peace too in Vietnam.

138

Chop off the heads of everybody who doesn't agree with them, doesn't want their system, especially the teachers. What they want the kids to learn is only one thing: hate, hate, hate. Do they care that drumming this into their heads will put millions of them in their graves? Seems to me, from what I read, that I am more worried about this than they are. They are loaded with kids. So what if ten million of them will be blown up in the final war of liberation? Hundred million? Five hundred million? Afterward, there will be a beautiful world of only Communists, maybe the new ones will be born with two heads, account of the radiation, but the real monsters, the imperialists, like the ones who are wrapping Care packages, will be kaput. And they can build the workers' paradise where everybody has a Chinese Cadillac. What I wish for them is that they should have our traffic problems with it."

"You used a word, Mr. Seidman. Talking about the children. You said 'worried.'"

"I don't mean worried. I'm not going around feeling worried for those Red Guards. It's the S.S. all over again, turned loose by their rotten government. They can go to hell. Don't twist my words."

"I have to deal with the words you use. Don't you think we may have a warped idea about what really goes on there?"

"And their idea about us? That's not warped?"

"Maybe there's some hope for better understanding on both sides, since Nixon's visit."

"Sure! Because they sat down to a couple of banquets and exchanged toasts, with all the fine words that slide out of politicians' mouths, like syrup from a barrel, every time they turn on the tap? And from twenty hours of talking privately, they issue a communiqué saying they didn't agree about anything except that it would be a good idea to start building a bridge to normal relations? And what are normal relations for Communists? That you should let them have their way in everything, and if not, that you should drop dead as soon as possible.

"Have you heard any word that they've changed the school-books, where every day millions of children read, like a prayer, that Mao is the sun and the moon and the stars; every day they learn that Jehovah-Mao says the United States is an imperialist demon and they must train themselves night and day to destroy the demon, and part of the gymnastic exercises for six- and eight-year-olds is to practice throwing wooden hand grenades? Tell me they've changed any of this since Nixon's visit and I'll tell you if I've got any hope for some understanding with these fanatics."

"But you said you were worried about them. The children. If you didn't mean worried, tell me what you did mean. Afraid?"

"Sure I'm afraid. In ten, twenty years, the old men like Chou who've still got a little judgment and can think about consequences will be dead and these brainwashed kids will be full-grown storm troopers, with enough nuclear missiles to wipe the imperialist enemy off the earth once and for all. Why shouldn't I be afraid? I've got an imperialist grand-daughter who's maybe growing up just to be vaporized. But what I am, more than afraid, is disgusted. I'm ashamed to be a member of the human race. If I could turn back evolution, I would stop where we were only tigers, or hyenas. They are an ornament on the earth, compared to us. And I'm sick of talking about this already. Let's talk about something else."

"So," the doctor says, "you've had your little orgy and you don't want to discuss it. You don't want me to say, for instance, that if China's leaders have hated and feared us, it's with considerable justification. You don't want me to suggest that for every act of violence, or hate, there is somewhere in the world we've made a countervailing act of mercy, or kindness, or generosity. Who should know that better than you, a kind and merciful and generous man? But at the moment you're on an emotional binge of rage and self-deprecation and the last thing you want from me is the black coffee of reason."

He sat looking at me for a minute while I tried to think of something to answer him back, and couldn't. "You're a new experience for me, Seidman," he said finally. "In the relatively short time you've been 'taking' from me, as you put it, you've managed to make me break most of the rules. You may send me back to my own analyst for a refresher course in how to conduct an analysis. In any case, I'm about to do something highly unorthodox. I'm about to tell you what I think is bothering you. And I'm prepared to see you leave, and never see you again."

"This would be a relief to you, I suppose."

"No, it wouldn't. I'd like to see you through to an understanding of your depression, see you released to do something affirmative, rewarding, with what's left of your life."

"Then don't talk about my leaving, please. We had an understanding about that."

"I believe your suggestion was that we might play pinochle, for the hour."

"I made progress since then. Believe it or not."

"All right. Here goes. It's my guess that your depression, disgust, feeling rotten as you say, stems from a realization that you're going to die, without ever doing most of the things you think would have given your life some importance, some stature."

I knew the minute he said it that it was somewhere near

141

the truth. And I didn't want to run, or tell him he was crazy.

"You profess to think that life has no meaning for you and you'd just as soon it ended. But actually you're in a rage about death, which you're probably facing for the first time in your life."

He waits to see what kind of reaction he's going to get from me. Maybe he really thought I would jump up and run away. But I was only thinking there's a lot of truth in what he said, and why couldn't I see this myself, without his telling me.

"You're in good company," he says when he sees I'm not going to open my mouth. "Do you read poetry?"

"I read a lot of it when I was young," I said. "Corny things. 'The Prisoner of Chillon.' 'The Ancient Mariner.' 'The Ballad of Reading Gaol.' The modern stuff I can't understand. I gave up trying."

"Dylan Thomas has written some lines, probably his best known, that I think you'll appreciate. 'Do not go gentle into that good night . . . Rage, rage against the dying of the light.' "

"This is about dying."

"Yes."

"He should have recited this to my father," I said. "He went like the company just shut off the gas and he was too tired to put another quarter in the meter. Could you say it again, please?"

He recited it over and I said, "Got a good sound to it. Strong."

"Yes. It's very good poetry. But very bad counsel for a rational human being. Thomas drank himself to death. I gather you're not a drinking man but you're doing pretty well in your own way. You've immobilized yourself, at a time when you should be active, productive, doing some good

142

in the world, or at least enjoying yourself and all your manifold blessings."

He got up. "Now if you don't mind, I'm going to cut this session a little short. You've given me a headache, the first in a long time. I'd like a few minutes in which to pull myself together for my next patient. Get back to being a practicing psychoanalyst, instead of a debater, a semanticist and a Dutch uncle, rolled into one."

The other night I had a dream. One of my problems with the analysis, Dr. Vogel says, is that I know a little bit about it from reading and I think I know a lot. Probably he's right, I know a little bit about many things from reading, what I don't know is the meaning of anything, and why should it be different with the analysis? But this dream, I couldn't see how it was from anxiety, or it was wish fulfillment or whatever, it was just a dream, from memory. Not a jumbled-up mishmash, the doctor loves to force me to take this kind apart, piece by piece, like a Chinese puzzle and put it together again so at the end there's some unbelievable conclusion, like for instance, the dream is that I'm listening to the record player at home, let's say Paganini's Perpetual Motion on the violin and I go get my old violin from the closet, and play along with it, note for note, perfect, and when it's finished I take the violin and like with a club I smash the record and the record player and the violin to pieces, and from this comes the idea that all my life I wanted to be a Heifetz on the violin. The doctor doesn't make this deduction, I got to make it myself and feel like a fool afterward.

But this was a different kind of dream, the kind you watch like an old movie on the Late Show, only the same time it's passing through your mind like on a screen, it's also going through your stomach or wherever the emotions are stored

143

away, like it would be a soundtrack of your feelings playing along for an accompaniment. You are like two people at the same time, the one who is watching and the one who is playing a part in the movie.

It was in the flat we used to live in on Delancey Street, over the poultry store. I saw there my mother and father, my sister Bessie and my brother Abe, we were all sitting around the kitchen table. I could see the room very clear, the gas mantel hanging over the table, the linoleum on the floor with the rusty places where it was worn out, and the wooden icebox and the window with the bars across it. It's hard for me now to believe this was to keep anybody out; I've got to remind myself there were people then who, if they could get a dollar for some stolen bedding or an old suit in a second-hand store, they could buy food for a few days, or maybe cigarettes or dope, who knows, like the kids today who knock down old ladies so they could get a handbag with six dollars in it, and they risk going to jail for ten years for this.

Or maybe the bars were mostly to keep the tenants from getting out when they got too far behind in the rent. Maybe you don't believe it but people lived this way, moving out, with wheelbarrows and pushcarts, in the middle of the night, two, three times a year. This was not our style; the worst thing in the world for my mother and father was to have debts and not be able to pay them. It ate them up alive, and I don't know how, but my mother would always somehow manage with the rent and the grocery bills.

The scene I'm telling you now, from the dream, was on a Friday night when my mother would try to push away the worries and have something special on the table for *Shabbas,* usually a chicken from the poultry store downstairs, with maybe a *tsimmes,* or a potato *kugel,* and there was always the

144

prayer over the candles. I don't think my parents were really religious. It was more habit, these observances, maybe a fear to break the tradition — I know, myself, something in the memory stays with you, demands your respect, even though you don't believe — the way I still go to services on the high holidays, and say *kaddish* for my father, after all these years.

Well, in the dream, even though I knew it was Friday night, there was no food on the table. We were just sitting, my mother's face was pale, more than usual, Bessie was in a high chair, banging on the tray with a broken rattle, my brother Abe was looking at a wallet in his hand and my father's face was red, this is not the way I usually remember him, mostly his complexion was green, with sad eyes, but now he was angry and he was hollering.

"This is all that falls into your head?" he was yelling at me. "To buy presents, with the first money you ever earned in your life? You don't know that we got rent to pay, that we got installments to pay, and gas and coal and grocery bills to pay? Cigars and cologne water," he yells and he picks up some cigars from the table in front of him and throws them on the floor, and then a bottle of cologne from in front of where my mother was sitting, and he throws this down too so it smashes on the floor, and then he jumps up and runs out of the house, slamming the door so hard the whole room shook from it, and Bessie started to cry. And I'm just sitting there, stunned, with a feeling in my stomach I couldn't describe, sick, but in a way you could never cure by vomiting, more like you would have swallowed some kind of slow poison and maybe you'll never get better from it, even though you wouldn't die.

This what I just told was the dream. But now I've got to tell what actually happened, what the dream was about. It

145

came back to me the next day, all the details, like it would have happened the week before. And actually it was, what? — forty-five years. Unbelievable. I was eleven. It was holiday time, I remember, Easter, for us *erev Pesach* — before Passover — I had a few days off from school and I got a job delivering, for a florist. Twelve to six, I remember, more often it was seven or eight, and all day Sunday. I wasn't allowed to work Saturday because my mother said, regardless if it was a sin or not (at eleven I was already beginning to ask questions, in those days it wasn't in my mind what I could do for God but I wondered a lot about what was He doing for us, and what was all the praying for, the *bruchas* and the breast beating, what were these people guilty of, except being poor) well, my mother said that even if it wasn't a sin to work on Saturday, it wasn't nice that the Gentiles should see a Jewish boy not having respect for the religion of his people. I think if I had a religion ever in my life, it was believing that what my mother said and did was the truest and best anybody could do in this world.

I was paid by the florist, I remember, fifty cents a day, and seventy-five for Sunday. On this Friday, that the dream was about, I had a delivery to make in Brooklyn Heights and the lady who got the flowers was very happy with them, she looked at the card and she did something funny, she threw out her arms and gave me a hug, with the flowers together, and then she said, "Wait a minute," and she went back in the house and came back with her purse. She looked inside for some change but she couldn't find any, so finally she took out a dollar and gave it to me. I couldn't believe it, and I remember I felt ashamed. Nowadays, it's part of how we live, the tipping, and I don't think about it anymore, but I never liked it, the idea, actually. I guess I felt it takes away something from a person, his dignity or something.

Anyway, I was standing there like a dummy and she took

146

my hand and put the dollar in it and said, "Don't be a fool, sonny, anybody offers you money, you take it, it's the most important commodity in the world." Seems to me, remembering the expression on her face when she saw the flowers, she had in mind something else that was the most important commodity in the world. But I didn't say anything then, it would surprise you, I know, how hard it was for me to open my mouth with people when I was a kid, I only became a big talker in later years. You're a little bit responsible, you know, you got me started that day long ago, in the park, the way you reacted I began to think maybe I'm really a *chochem*, a smart fellow, and a humorist too, and I haven't got over it since.

Well, dignity shmignity, a dollar was a fortune those days and twice I couldn't refuse. Afterward, I was walking down the street to the subway station and I had my hand in my pocket closed around the dollar bill and all of a sudden I felt like drunk with wealth, power, I don't know what. I've made a lot of money since then, lost some too, but I tell you I never had the feeling what it is to have money, to be rich, like I did that day. Believe me, Rockefeller had nothing on me. We were in the same club. Except there's a story that Rockefeller, the old man, gave away dimes when he was feeling generous, and I was feeling much richer than that. It fell into my head that instead of I should walk into the house that evening like always and say, Ma, what's for supper, I'm hungry, I would come in like Harun al-Rashid from the Arabian Nights, with presents for everybody, and I went to a Woolworth's on Atlantic Avenue and got the cologne and the rattle and the wallet, and then I went to a United Cigar Store and bought four White Owl cigars for a quarter, and told the man to wrap them nice with a piece of ribbon I also bought in Woolworth's.

Then I went back to the florist, he was a Greek and he talked with a heavy accent and between the Yiddish and the

English running around in my head it was a hard job for me sometimes to understand him. I remember I asked him if he read the Sayings of Epictetus and he told me not to be such a smart little greenhorn and to keep my mind on the deliveries. Anyway, he wanted to know what took me so long, just to Brooklyn Heights, but he gave me my fifty cents for the day and this too I put in a special envelope I bought in Woolworth's, it had like a gold edging all around.

I was very excited, you understand, going home. I knew that by now everybody would be at the table, waiting for supper. I came in, not saying a word, not even hello, good *Shabbas*, nothing. I put the envelope with the fifty cents in front of my mother, with the bottle of cologne, wrapped fancy with silver paper and ribbon, and the rattle I put on the highchair for Bessie, and the wallet in a box for Abe and the cigars in front of my father and I sat down and waited for everybody to say, My goodness, look what this boy has done, thank you, hurray for Prince *Mashe* (that's the Jewish name for Morris). Instead everybody is unwrapping the things, without a word, except Bessie, there was no paper around the rattle so she starts to *hock* with it on the highchair and in ten seconds it's broken. Everybody else just sits, looking at the things until my father said, looking at the cigars, "What did you pay for these ropes?"

Not exactly what I expected him to say. Took me a minute to open my mouth. "A quarter," I said. "In the United Cigar Store. I got coupons too."

"Where did you get the money to buy these things, Mashe?" my mother said.

"I didn't steal it," I told her. "A rich lady in Brooklyn Heights gave it to me."

My father is looking at the cigars. "A quarter," he said. He looked up at me and I see he's starting to get red in the

148

face. "You know what a quarter is? It's gas for lights and cooking, for a week. It's a payment for the Prudential. It's meat for supper for two days. What are you, an idiot? The first money you make in your life you throw it away on this *dreck?*"

Well, my mother tried to make him stop but he was yelling like he would never stop and I was sitting there with this sickness in my stomach I couldn't describe, and finally my father jumped up from the table, like I said, and threw the cigars and cologne on the floor and went out of the house, slamming the door. The rest of us just sat there, not looking at each other. Finally my brother, Abe, said, "It's all right, Mashe, you're a born sport. Pa can't understand that, he's got his nose stuck in the wheels of that pushcart all the time."

Poor Abe, he was a sport too, he got mixed up with a gang there on the East Side a few years later, and one day they took him out of a poolroom, his head smashed in from a cue, and he died on the way to the Emergency.

My mother said to me finally, "Mashe, go find your father, bring him back."

"No," I said. "I don't want to talk to him. I'll never talk to him again in my whole life."

So she pulled me to her and smoothed back my hair and said, "You got to try to understand, Masheleh. What you did, it's very nice, but you are eleven years old and he is a man nearly forty and this is what he would like to do, bring presents *erev Pesach,* but he can't. So he hollers. Go. Find him and tell him we're waiting with supper."

Well, I didn't want to, I just had my heart cut out and it didn't seem fair I should have to go to my father now and apologize to him because I'm bleeding. But when my mother said something it was like law, not because she was strict but

149

because even if you couldn't understand it at the time, you knew in your insides she was always right. I went downstairs and my father was sitting on the stoop next door, and he was crying. I couldn't understand it. First he's mad at me and screaming, now he's crying, and I stood there, not feeling sorry for him, I was very hurt you understand; after all, I could have used the money for malted milks, this was a passion with me when I was a kid, malted milks for eight cents, and those little blue books, I'd discovered them by then, I could have bought ten and had enough left over for a malted every day for a week. Instead, I made a sacrifice, for the family, the first time I ever had a chance, and what comes of it. The cologne is spilled, the rattle is broken in two seconds, the wallet for Abe will be in the hockshop tomorrow and my father instead of lighting one of the cigars and saying thanks, it's delicious, you're a loving and thoughtful son, yells at me like I would have been a criminal with the money.

He looks up and sees me. I didn't know what to say to him but he pulled me down on the stoop and held me in his arms, rocking a little. And he said, "I'm sorry, Mashe, I didn't mean to holler, not at you, I don't know who I was hollering at, but not you. I'm ashamed. I'm ashamed."

"Why, Papa?" I said. "I didn't take the money from anybody. A lady gave it to me because she was happy, and I thought you would be happy — "

"I know, I know. I'm scared of this America, Mashe, it was bad in the old country but this is worse, to be a failure here, where people got dollars to hand out for tips and I couldn't make enough to take care of the family."

And all of a sudden I understood the whole thing. I said, "It's all right, Papa, I'll make enough for all of us, wait and see." And I tried to smile but then I was crying too, with him.

Well, you wouldn't believe it, my friend, but when I told

this whole story to the doctor — don't forget, like I said, this happened more than forty years ago — all of a sudden, in the middle of talking I had to stop, because I got choked up and I knew if I would say one more word, I would be crying, like that kid on the stoop. Can you imagine how ridiculous, a man fifty-five, a pillow in the community like my sister Bessie says, I'm older now than my father was when he died, and I got to fight away the tears, like it all happened yesterday, and I'm still the same boy in mended pants?

After a while I hear Vogel say, "What occurs to you about this dream?"

This is the technique, of course, used to drive me crazy in the beginning but I'm used to it by now that whenever the conversation between us stops for a minute and I got nothing to say, or nothing I want to say, he gives me this little push. "What occurs to you?"

"Occurs to me," I said, "that whoever figured out this life has got a rotten sense of humor."

"Come on, Seidman," he says, "that kind of remark isn't worthy of you."

"I thought you said in analysis, the doctor doesn't make judgments."

He sits back, looks at me for a minute, pulling his nose. Then he says, "I thought you understood by now that this is not an analysis by the book. You don't need an analysis, Seidman. You're not sick. You're woefully self-indulgent at this point, and that's the main thing we have to deal with. Now stop debating with me and let's talk about this dream."

"What's to say," I said. "You want the truth? I still feel like bawling when I think of my father sitting there on the stoop, telling me he's ashamed. The poor *shnook*. He wasn't supposed to know about making a living, a big entrepreneur of shoelaces and safety pins. He was supposed to be a scholar, a teacher. All around him people were making out, with the pushcarts, because they were sharp to figure out what were the specialty items for the neighborhood, or they knew how to buy job lots cheaper than regular, or they would make deals to handle stolen merchandise, or bootleg cigarettes — what did my father know about such things? Somebody would come to him with a proposition about stolen goods, first he would faint a little, then he would holler, then if it was a Jewish boy who was making him the proposition he would worry he shouldn't end up in jail, or if it was an Italian he would worry about the Black Hand and not sleep nights.

"The man was a big *shlemiel,* let's face it, he was like somebody from another world got dropped on Delancey Street. The best thing could happen to him during the day was for some other *shlemiel* to come along and they should talk about Spinoza or how many lies there were in the Bible, or if Lenin was a bigger bastard, or Trotski."

"You made him a sort of promise, that day on the stoop," the doctor said. " 'I'll make enough for all of us, wait and see.' Did you keep the promise?"

"Of course. Would I break a promise like this? A year later, when I was twelve, I went to work in a skirt factory as a shipping clerk and two years later, when I was fourteen, I already worked myself up to apprentice cutter, which I could do when I wasn't *shlepping* around bolts of material, or wrapping boxes. My salary was eight dollars a week and I moved the family to a ten-room apartment on Park Avenue, with a doorman and hot and cold running elevators. The reason I could do this is because I only kept out from the eight dollars enough for carfare and a Vienna roll and a glass of milk for lunch. And sometimes a Haldemann-Julius book for a nickel."

"All right, Seidman. Don't get off the track."

152

"The track is I never did a goddam thing for him. Not for him or for my mother. Because by the time I was starting to make even a little bit of a success they were both dead and buried."

"And now you feel guilty."

"I don't feel guilty. I feel like smashing something, or somebody who loaded on these people a lifetime of poverty and misery, putting on every day a little more, pushing them into the ground little by little with worry and sickness, until finally they had only a little bit more to go before the dirt could be thrown on them to cover them over, get them out of sight. For what? What did they do? What was their crime?"

"That's a question you could ask about a lot of people, Seidman."

"All right, so I'm asking. You got an answer? The answer is it's all nonsense, the whole thing. That's already the *best* it could be. Because if it's something else, not nonsense, if somebody figured out it should be like this, if there's somebody or something responsible, it's so terrible to think about it, you could only lose your mind or kill yourself."

"Or recognize that it's part of *our* responsibility, being sentient, being what we call human, to do what we can to ameliorate." Before I could say anything back to this, he said, "Tell me about your job in the skirt factory."

"What should I tell you? It was a big adventure, from morning to night. In the beginning, as an apprentice cutter, my job was to lay out lengths of material from the bolts, and take care of the remnants and between times deliver packages. After a while, I learned how to handle the big shears and follow the markings made from the patterns by the head cutter. Then finally they let me use the new electric cutting machine and the first thing I did was slice off a piece of my finger. Just a little piece but it's still missing, you could see.

This didn't happen because I was careless, but because I'm also a *shlemiel,* partly by inheritance I suppose, and in those days, besides, my head was full of poetry and philosophy from those little blue books and I would stand like in a trance at the cutting table, saying over in my mind a poem or some wonderful lines that I read the night before, or on the subway coming to work — sometimes I would forget the sandwich my mother fixed for me to take along for lunch, but never one of the little books in my pocket.

"You know, it's still a peculiar pleasure for me, looking through the carton of nickel treasures I've kept from forty years ago, they are my alma mater, I remind myself how I got an education from them, nickel by nickel. What feasts. I was maybe nine, ten years old when I started to collect them, sometimes I didn't know exactly what I was reading, it was just the music, the magic of the words, the marvelous new language. I tell you, I had such a feeling those days — I was a patriot, doctor, a true patriot. America the Beautiful was what was in my mind all the time. Had nothing to do with the facts. I didn't know the facts. What did I know about Sacco and Vanzetti, *their* beautiful America, the I.W.W., the fights of the garment workers for decent hours and wages; I didn't know that there was a depression coming, I didn't care that I got a rock in the head if I went sometimes the wrong way home, that I was a kike, a sheeny, a green-horn, that I had to bring every cent home and figure out, sometimes not so kosher, how to get the nickels for the little books. Every month at rent time there was a crisis in the family — didn't matter, any of it — it wore out my father and put my mother, thirty-eight years old, in her grave — but for me nothing could squash the feeling that this was a whole new world opening up for me, not commerce, skyscrapers, Wall Street, the West — the Sayings of Marcus Aurelius, five

154

cents, with a roll and a glass of milk, ten cents, the Essays of Montaigne, the plays of Shakespeare, the poems of Swinburne, Byron, Shelley — I drank them in like wine and why I don't know, but I got from them always the feeling I was going to be *somebody,* nothing was going to stop me.

"Well, this day, I don't remember who was responsible, Shakespeare or Byron or Marcus Aurelius, but there was a piece of my finger on the goods, and some blood too which was more important, the boss was horrified, he pushed me away before the blood could soak through to the next layer, then he sent me to a doctor. It was about a mile away from the shop and nobody thought to ask me if I had a nickel for carfare so I walked, with a piece of newspaper wrapped around the finger. When I got to the doctor's office it was full of people. I didn't know what to do so I sat down, holding the finger in the newspaper and after a while the blood soaked through and started to drip on the floor. A nurse came over and scolded me and she got a saucer, or an ashtray, I don't remember which, and told me to hold my finger over it and not mess up the rug. I've thought about that nurse sometimes, over the years. You couldn't say she was a Florence Nightingale type. More like Madame Defarge. She could at least have got me a fresh piece of newspaper.

"Finally the doctor took me in his office and bandaged me up, he was very nice, gave me a little brandy to drink and told me to pay the nurse on the way out, and when I told her I didn't have any money to pay she started hollering, I thought I would end up in jail altogether.

" 'That's always how it is with you little kikes,' she yelled, 'you always expect to get everything for nothing.' Well, the upshot was — and you'll say, I bet, when you read this, that I'm making it up but I swear it's the truth — my boss paid the doctor and the end of the week when I got my salary, there was a slip deducting for the doctor and besides this, docking me the three hours I was out of the shop.

"It was a good experience for me, in a way, because when I got a shop of my own, years later, I never hated the union like some of my competitors. No matter how much aggravation they gave me, and it was plenty over the years, I was always two people fighting with the delegate. One was the kid who could have used a union, or the government or somebody against that son of a bitch of a boss. Makes my blood boil when I think of it now. He was a real kosher Jew too, we couldn't work on Saturdays, he opened the shop half an hour earlier on Sunday instead."

"You've told me," the doctor said, "you always had the feeling in those days that you were going to be *somebody*. That's the word you used. What gave you that feeling?"

"I don't know. What gives people the idea they are going to heaven when they die? Or that they could write a great book, if only they had the time. Or discover a cure for cancer if somebody had only put them in a laboratory instead of a haberdashery store. This is the dream, I talked to you about this already. Keeps you hypnotized, going round and round with the machinery, like a horse."

"Horses don't dream, Seidman."

"How do you know? Did you ever analyze a horse?"

"I had a patient a few years ago, a young woman, who used to dream about being a horse."

"Don't tell me the dream came true and now she's winning races in the Derby?"

He doesn't even smile. With this man, I could never make a reputation as a humorist. "I shouldn't have said that," he says. "As a matter of fact there's some work being done now that suggests that animals *do* dream."

"Wouldn't surprise me that a horse should dream about

156

being an automobile, or a hyena should dream about having a rosy behind, like a mandrill. It's a beautiful looney bin, this world, where everyone wants to be something that he's not."

"You've talked a good deal about music in our sessions. Have you ever wanted to play a musical instrument? Tried to?"

"When I was a kid one of the dreams was to give Heifetz a run for his money. When I could afford it I bought a violin and I took some lessons."

"How did it go?"

"I found out I was lucky I went in the dress business."

He looks at his watch. "We've run out of time," he says. "I'd like you to think about something between now and our next session. Maybe it's not just sorrow you feel for your father. Maybe there's some anger mixed up in your feelings, some resentment that he wasn't stronger, more resourceful, to make his way against the odds, like many others did in the same circumstances. To make a better life for his family. And maybe because this is a hidden resentment you feel, or felt, toward a man whose lot was certainly difficult and for whom you also feel pity, perhaps what's emerged from these confused emotions is a sense of guilt which you are now expiating by turning *yourself* into a *shlemiel,* letting your fine intelligence, your curiosity, your creative capacities go by the board, while you luxuriate — "

"Again, luxuriate?"

"Yes. Luxuriate in the feeling of being useless, impotent, defeated — using as an excuse the dictum that everything is nonsense, life is an empty dream — "

"Wait a minute," I said. "You're going to tell me now life is real, life is earnest and the grave is not its goal? This is what the whole analysis is going to end up with? That ter-

157

rible poem? I hated it when I had to learn it in night school, I hated the teacher, I hated Longfellow — "

"Well, you can hate me too," he says. "Just the same, think about what I've said."

I thought about it. Not because I wanted to, I couldn't help myself. I was angry with him at first, furious, this was the real analytic *dreck,* that stupid parlor game with the secret language — I'm sorry for my father but I'm not really sorry, actually I hate him and resent him — but I couldn't enjoy myself resenting him because I also feel pity for him, and finally I feel guilty because I resent — well, I tried to put it out of my mind but I couldn't. It was like he gave me a spin, like a top, when I left his office, and I couldn't help twirling around, making myself dizzy. Not to say crazy.

But a funny thing. Gradually, it started to make sense to me, what he said. And now I got to tell you a really funny thing. I left the office early that afternoon, Vangie wasn't in the shop and I didn't feel like sitting down to write what happened just then, so I got home in the afternoon and the first thing I did was to get out my violin from the closet where I keep it. I haven't touched it, I mean to play, for I don't know how many years. The strings were all right and I tuned it up and started to play "Traümerei." Not exactly in tune and the bow slid around a little but wasn't too bad.

After a while Sophie came in, with packages, what else, and she said, "I heard you, coming down the hall."

"So," I said.

"So if this is the result of the analysis and you're going back to becoming a violinist in your riper years, maybe I'll take the whole thing back. Better quit and go back to moping."

But she was joking. I'm not the only one in the family. Or

maybe she caught it from me, by osmosis. She came over and gave me a kiss, and said, "Play, gypsy, play. Only let me make sure all the windows are closed. I don't want the neighbors to get jealous."

"Doctor," I said, "do you think I could commit murder?"

"Under sufficient provocation anybody is capable of murder. I'd say the likelihood in your case is small. Are you thinking of killing someone?"

"I wish I had the nerve."

"Who is it you'd like to kill?"

"An Armenian son of a bitch."

"Your daughter's friend?"

"Yes."

"Am I to assume that his wife won't divorce him?"

"He hasn't got a wife."

"Really? You want to tell me about it," he said, "or shall I keep digging? Like an archaeologist."

"Ah ha," I said. "I gave you a weapon with which you could attack me. Archaeology."

"Is it a touchy subject for you? You described it as fascinating."

"I know what you're trying to do. You're trying to *mishel* me around so I'll start talking about Vangie."

"That wasn't what I had in mind. But if you'd like to talk about Vangie, I think it might lead to some clarification of your feelings about her."

"I was talking about Jenny."

"I know. Don't you sometimes feel there's a connection between them in your mind?"

"You're going to tell me now I've got incestuous feelings about my daughter."

"Seidman, every father has incestuous feelings about his

159

daughters. Every man alive has had homosexual fantasies. Every man alive has felt the desire to murder. The difference between healthy and sick is how the individual deals with these impulses. And maturity manifests itself in acknowledging them and not feeling impelled to run and hide from them behind Mama's apron, as from the boogieman. You've got me giving a lecture again," he said. But he smiled.

I sat and thought about what he just said. Sometimes it's more than you could get down in one gulp.

"Well," he said, "do you want to tell me about Jenny?"

"I had a visit from her yesterday, in the shop. When the receptionist called to say she was there, I couldn't believe it. 'Send her in,' I said. 'If she still remembers the way to my office.' She came in and I took ten seconds' pleasure from the way she looked. I didn't dare to take more because I know, with Jenny, I'll pay dear later on for every second of pleasure she gives me."

I stopped and looked at the doctor. "What is that expression on your face?"

"You want to know what I was thinking."

"Yes. If I'm not being too personal."

"I was wondering why people don't treat life as an adventure, instead of an exercise in cost accounting."

"Could you explain that a little?"

"You took pleasure in your daughter's appearance. Why didn't you let it go at that, instead of spoiling it for yourself by anticipating something disastrous to follow. Time enough to count the cost later, isn't it?"

"You could be right. But I'm always scared, with Jenny, that she'll give me something to think about that will turn my stomach upside down."

"Did she?"

"I'll give you the conversation. 'Hello, Pa,' she said, 'I was in the neighborhood, I thought I'd drop in. You want to take me to lunch?' Well, this hasn't happened for years. So again I figured, it's got to be something really bad she's going to tell me. Then I heard her say, 'Pa, I'm not pregnant.' "

I saw a smile come on the doctor's face. The second time today. "What did you say to that?" he asked me.

"I said, 'how do you know?' 'What do you mean, how do I know,' she says. 'I've got another question for you, Jenny,' I said. 'Why didn't you wait until I asked you.'

" 'Well,' she says, 'you had that look on your face.' You see we are all clairvoyant, doctor, the whole Seidman family. 'What look?' I said.

" 'The My-God-she's-pregnant look,' " she says.

The doctor laughed now. Actually laughed. "You think this is funny?" I said.

"I think your daughter is a girl I'd take pleasure in, if I were her father."

"Sure," I said. "From the sidelines it's easy."

"What happened next?" he said. Waiting for another laugh, I guess.

"I said, 'Jenny, how would you like to go out and come back in again, say hello, and maybe we can have a conversation like normal people, with words, sentences, not with you translating my looks.'

" 'I'm sorry,' she said. 'Let's have lunch. I've got a story to tell you I think you'll appreciate.' Well, appreciate is a good word but I don't know if it fits exactly. The story she told me is this executive she is going with is not married, it's just something he invented to protect himself from girls trying to move in. And the night before, when Jenny had a date with him, he called up and said he was tied up with a very important business meeting and he was sending a good friend of his, whom he was sure she'd like, to substitute for him.

" 'Isn't that nice?' Jenny said. 'Such a considerate man. He wanted to be sure I wouldn't be stuck with a wasted evening, no sex or anything. I guess the next move is for me to have some cards printed.'

" 'Would you like to get your face slapped here in this restaurant?' I said. You know what she did? She blew me a kiss.

" 'You still care, don't you,' she said.

" 'Why don't *you* care, Jenny?' I said. 'The way you are living. No standards, no rules — '

" 'I've got my own rules, Pa. They're just not yours.'

" 'What are you going to do about this man?'

" 'Well, I thought of going to his office and sticking a paper knife in his throat.'

" 'Maybe I will do it for you,' I said.

" 'No,' she said, 'he's not important enough. It's funny, I didn't figure on anything permanent with him. He's not someone I planned to spend the rest of my life with. I've got another model in mind for that.'

" 'Who?' I said.

"She gave me a funny look. 'Marcus Aurelius,' she said. 'But Derek is so convinced he's God's gift to women, and so terrified of any commitment, he just couldn't believe I didn't want anything from him but an honest relationship, for as long as it lasted. With no small print in the deal. He had to put up a barricade of lies and then when he felt himself getting more emotionally involved with me than was safe, the only thing he could do to deny my importance to him was to put me down, send one of his toadies around to prove I was just another pushover.'

"Some word. Pushover. How could I have dreamed, doctor, when I was listening to this girl give the valedictory address in her high school that this is the kind of conversation I would be having with her just a few years later."

"Seems like pretty good conversation to me," Dr. Vogel

162

said. "But let's not debate that. I want to hear the rest of this."

"You heard what's important. I said something foolish, I suppose, that I would like to pay this man off some way. And she said, 'Why bother? He's a sick man, Pa. He'll end his days in emptiness. I feel sorry for him, actually. But I don't intend to waste any time over that either. I just wanted to tell you about it.'

" 'Why, Jenny?'

" 'Because I know my seeing him has been bugging you and I thought you'd like to know it's over.' Then she gave me a look, reminded me of when she was a little girl, telling me what we used to call a fib. My God, what a different world. Fib. Whoever thought then that the right word is bullshit.

" 'That's not the real reason, Pa,' Jenny said. 'It's because I wanted to talk about this to someone I love. And who loves me.'

"Well, doctor, this is maybe not the best way to find out you've still got a relationship with your daughter but it's better than to think it just fell into a hole one day, when you weren't looking, and disappeared forever.

" 'You're pretty foxy,' I said to her. 'How could I scold you now?'

" 'Do you want to?' she said. 'I'll listen.'

" 'No. But maybe you learned from this experience a lesson, Jenny.'

" 'Yes,' she said. 'I'm never again going to get mixed up with a Rumanian TV executive who speaks Oxford English and is grooming himself to be a character in a Jacqueline Susann novel.' "

Again I heard the doctor laugh. A red letter day. "You like this story," I said.

"I like the girl in it."

163

"You think it was perfectly all right she should sleep with a married man."

"But he's not married."

"She didn't know that. She thought he was."

"Seidman, your wife sleeps with a married man," he said. "My wife sleeps with a married man."

"You picked a fine time to make jokes," I said.

"Forgive me for trespassing on your domain. You must remember, Seidman, we analysts are widely regarded as depraved characters who encourage licentiousness and lewdness and such-like traffickings with the devil."

"You're in a funny mood today, doctor."

"I'm in a good mood. I like to hear about young people who are making it, against all the odds."

"You're talking about Jenny? You don't think this is a degrading thing that happened to her?"

"It would have been, if she let herself be degraded by it. But she didn't."

"Could this have happened if there were some standards left in the world, how girls should behave? Some decency — "

"Decency is something within, Seidman. I congratulate you on a daughter who appears to have a sizable fund of it. And a lot of good sense besides. I know you'll hate to hear this but you have to take some of the responsibility."

A funny session.

IV

This week Vangie is away for the Easter holiday, to visit her parents in Canada. Dr. Vogel is also away for a psychiatric conference somewhere, so I got nobody to talk to and if it wasn't for this journal, or whatever it is I'm keeping, I would really go crazy. You can imagine my condition, I even considered for a minute to go up to my club and play golf. But it passed away, I guess I'm really not desperate.

Seriously, though, I didn't realize how much, lately, I got to look forward to my talks with Vangie, and how much I would miss them if she's not around. I found lately a way to spend time with her without making a situation at home, or getting looks from Harold because I take up too much of her time in the shop. I drive her to school when she's got afternoon classes. Sometimes I meet her after her morning classes and we have lunch. Or I come back in the afternoon when she is finished and we go for a drink.

You would think between her and the analyst I would have run out of talk already. But it's like an addiction with me, I guess. And the thing is, with Vangie, I listen a lot.

I wonder if sometimes she is talking for an effect, to see my reaction. The way I did with her when I made up the business about a girl friend. I told you I'm prepared that her way of looking at things is different than mine but she comes out occasionally with something that sounds so outrageous I don't know if I should believe she's serious or not. For instance, like she said to me the other day about marriage. It's a contract, she said, between two consenting adults for long-term suicide.

"Vangie," I said, "this is nonsense. You give me sometimes some hard nuts to crack, with your ideas. But this is just silly, what you said."

"Yes? Look at you," she said.

"Me? I'm dead, or what?"

"Not dead. Just maimed."

"How?"

"When were you on a trip last? Alone?"

"I don't like to travel alone. I told you. A hotel room by myself is to me like a coffin."

"So you've locked yourself into a prison, instead of a coffin. Nine rooms and four baths, one for the maid, very sumptuous. You'll never be sprung, and you don't want to be. That's the horror of the whole thing."

"You sound angry," I said.

"I *am* angry. You're a pussy cat, a charming, lovable pussy cat. You should have been a lion."

I laughed. I think it was a laugh. "Vangie, if I went home now and told my wife I'm going to Yucatán for a week, by myself, this would make me a lion?"

"You know what I'm talking about," she said. "You don't know what it means anymore to have an independent thought or impulse or desire. Or if you do, it trails off in wistfulness. Or depression."

"You make a very gloomy picture. I could show you another side."

"Sure. Pussy cats on Central Park West have lots of cream in their diets. I'll bet you've even got a corner where you can go scratch without marring the furniture. If your daughter hasn't appropriated it."

166

"Why are you so upset, Vangie?"

"I don't know. I guess it's all this pressure I've been getting about marriage."

"You could set your own pattern. It's only a contract after all. You could make your own terms."

"You can't, that's the point. It's like saying you can be a Catholic on your own terms. You accept the dogma, or you're excommunicated. Whatever resolves I made to start out with, I'd find myself slipping into the mold — that horrible symbiosis that creeps up on married people and turns them into joined jellyfish. Is there anything more sickening than the possessiveness of a loving wife? Like a female spider, endlessly having her mate and eating him too."

"You are really a Mohammedan, some part of you," I said. "But I wonder if you would be so happy, having to share."

"That's it. You've just said it. Share. Marriage is a claim two people stake out on each other. No sharing. Anyone jumps your claim, you've a right to shoot him dead. The unwritten law. The whole thing stinks. It ought to be abolished."

I never saw her before so worked up. She's wrong, of course. But it's the way young people think. Everything is either one way, or another. No middle way. No compromise, expediency, no settling for half, like Harold used to say. I suppose to be willing to settle for half, or less, is something you got to acquire with the years, like arthritis. It's a very clear thing for the young people to see there's a lot of politicians who are hypocrites and crooks. Who doesn't see this? But for them it's simple: throw out the government, the whole system. Dow Chemical makes napalm, shut down the whole chemical industry. Automobiles make pollution, so go back to bicycles. Modern society makes problems for people, psychological problems, not only smog and pollution —

167

alienation, depersonalization and so on — so go live in a commune and grow carrots for a living. Doesn't matter that it's somebody else's land, and you've got to get your seeds courtesy of the establishment you want to run away from, or destroy, and you can't live on carrots only — you are making your statement about how you want to live. And included in the statement, of course, has got to be an allowance for pot, ten dollars a sack.

Lots of marriages are no good, who could deny this, the statistics are there even if you haven't suffered yourself from social evenings where you've got to sit and watch a couple playing Virginia Woolf, a husband doing the Chinese torture of a thousand cuts, or a wife sitting coiled up like an anaconda, swallowing what's left of her husband — the thing is, so you've abolished marriage. What's next? Seems to me, only chaos. How many Vangies are there, with her looks, her mind, her character; you've got to be a very special person for the kind of independence she's talking about. It's not for everybody; the world God made is not a democracy, I don't care what the ADA says.

Probably it's true I turned into a pussy cat over the years. Jews in my generation had a good start in this direction. Those who wanted to be something else got their noses and their heads broken early; more often they turned into hyenas, not lions. So when the time came, I didn't write up a sign DOWN WITH MARRIAGE, HURRAY FOR FREE LOVE and parade in front of City Hall. I married the most beautiful girl in the world, like every other good Jewish boy; I was only too happy and grateful for the chance to sell my balls for a mess of Flatbush. (You know, I couldn't see anybody collecting the sayings of Ralphie, like I got in one of the little blue books the Sayings of Epictetus, but I've got to admit what he says sometimes sticks in the mind.) So I gave up my in-
168

dividuality, I'm not sure what it means. Seems to me the worst fate in the world would be every night to go to the door and say good night, or good-bye, and turn back to face an empty house.

Reminds me, I had a talk with Sophie the other night. She wanted also to go away for the holidays. "Let's go up to Grossinger's for a few days," she said. "The Gerbers are going. You like them."

"In very small portions," I said. "About twice a year, for two hours, maximum."

"Is there anybody you like to spend time with these days, Morris?"

"The only one I could think of, off hand, charges sixty dollars an hour."

"You used to like Grossinger's," she said.

"Lox and bagels and bagels and lox. I don't have to travel two hundred miles for this."

"You want to go to the club for a few days?"

"And play golf? No, thank you."

"Would you like to take a trip? Portugal? I understand there's a wonderful place, Algarve, beautiful beach, you could take along some books — "

"What about the analysis," I said. "You sent me to have an analysis. You want me to drop it now?"

"I want you to want to do something besides mope. You could take a leave of absence from your analyst for a few weeks. Isn't there *something* you'd like to do?"

"I would like you to stop pestering me about finding something I'd like to do. That's what I'd like."

Right away I was sorry I used that particular word. "Would you like *me* to go away?" she said, beginning to go into her coloratura range. I'm very much for this with Bev-

169

erly Sills but when Sophie does it I get nervous. "Would you like to go live by yourself where you won't have to listen to my pestering?"

What could I answer? I wanted to stop, I felt bad, but I couldn't say so just then. What I said was, "Don't get hysterical," and in case you want an advice from me how to deal with a woman who is getting hysterical, this is exactly what you shouldn't say.

"Just tell me what you want," she said; I would say she screamed, except Sophie doesn't scream. "You want to have an affair with somebody — *just tell me*," she said. "You've got *carte blanche*, Morris. Anything you want. Only not to turn into a dismal old man in front of my eyes."

She ran out of the room, I saw she was crying. I wanted to follow her, to comfort her. But I couldn't. I don't know why. Because I *felt* like a dismal old man? Because I would have to tell her some lies, some good resolutions I would make — in thirty years how many times do you do this kind of thing with a woman you care about?

But I have to ask myself, also, why didn't I tell Vangie about this conversation? Just let her go on with her foolish tirade about how I'm locked in a prison, with a wife who is my jailer.

I haven't written down anything the past few weeks, I've been too confused in my mind, what is the truth and what isn't. I guess the analyst is responsible, partly, he's got me into this new style, questioning every thought that goes through my head, like it would be a sneak thief trying to steal away my integrity. It would be a fine thing if now, after all these years telling you how I hate hypocrisy and pretense, I should start to cover up things or try to hide them because they don't make me look like such a hero. Dr. Vogel said something to me that comes to my mind more and more often; words could be used two ways, he said, to reveal and to disguise. And I see now how big is the temptation sometimes to run behind them from the truth.

If I want to be honest I've got to say I knew all along what was happening to me with Vangie. I could have stopped it, but I didn't want to. It's like I was keeping my back turned, so I wouldn't see this was something that was happening to me, not somebody else. If I couldn't see what was going on, I couldn't be responsible. This was the idea, I guess.

It's pretty mixed up. I wish you were here and I could talk to you. With Vogel it's no use. In one way, he's very good, doesn't let me get away with anything. But comes to a little help, he's not there. I've got to flounder around and find my own way. Or be lost in my own way, is more the situation. All I know for sure, it's very plain to me, is that in the beginning when I was with this girl, it was the only time I stopped wishing, secretly, that someone would make me a present of a heart attack from which I wouldn't get up.

What I told myself in the mirror was that I was interested to get some kind of an education, how young people think, so I would improve my relationship with my daughter. But if this was maybe true in the very beginning — and I'm not even sure of this now — it stopped being true very soon. When I was looking forward to being with Vangie, and sneakily making opportunities, behind my back, it wasn't to get an education in anything, it was because I love to listen to her, to hear her laugh, to see the expression changing in her eyes like light on a piece of taffeta.

Maybe you're wondering why I haven't mentioned something about Ralphie. It's not because I forgot about him, or he's not on my mind, believe me. I had a dream about him a few nights ago. We were in a coffee house, I was dressed very peculiar, in a velvet coat and a crazy bow tie, like you see in one of those Impressionist pictures of the artist and his friends in his studio, and I was wearing a Borsalino hat, a green one, I had one like it that I bought maybe twenty-five years ago, I haven't worn it for twenty. I was talking, very eloquent, there were some kids around listening and I was telling how in my day I was a socialist and everything the young people think is so new now that they are saying, about the system and the Establishment and free love and so on, we thought of it long before them and we didn't have to throw rocks at policemen and manure at college professors to show that we were sincere.

Ralphie was listening and suddenly he said, "You're an old fart, Unk, and if you ever believed in anything but a fast shuffle or fudging on your income tax, it was a hundred years ago and why don't you shut up and act your age."

I got so furious I jumped up and picked up a chair and threw it at him and instead of hitting him it went into a window and broke it and there was a big hoo-ha, the proprietor said he would put me in jail and I told him not to get excited and I wrote him a check. Then afterward Vangie came in and she told Ralph to apologize for what he said to me, and I was furious with her because she heard it, and I said to her, "Never mind butting in, Vangie, I was handling my own affairs before you were born and I don't need you to be my champion with my own nephew."

Then I was sick, actually sick in my stomach, because I thought after this way I talked to her I would never see her again.

A real mishmash of a dream. I didn't even tell it to Dr. Vogel. I've got to tell you now two things. First about the evening I was with Vangie and I forgot to watch the time and when I got home it was almost two o'clock. Sophie was still up, reading in bed.

"Why are you up?" I said.

"I was worried," she said. "You said you'd be home by twelve."

"It's okay," I said. "I don't have school tomorrow." I don't know why, maybe I felt guilty, but I sounded very cranky. I didn't want to, but I couldn't help myself.

She didn't change her voice. Sometimes, with Sophie, I wonder if she figures since she sent me to an analyst, she's got to treat me a little bit like a mental case. I noticed, since that explosion I wrote about, when she yelled at me to go away, to have an affair, to go to the devil, anything, since then she doesn't get upset. Or maybe she's upset and doesn't show it. I've got to believe it can't be easy for her lately, my moods and everything.

"Where were you so late?" she says, quiet.

"Why are you keeping such tabs on me, Sophie?" I said, not quiet. "With the time, and who, and what — what am I, on parole or something?"

"I'm not keeping tabs," she said. "Something could happen to a person in that jungle. Does it bother you that I still care about what happens to you?"

"I'm sorry. I had trouble to get a taxi."

"What happened to your car?"

"I couldn't get it started. The carburetor is clogged, or something. You want to examine it?"

"Tell me why you're so defensive, Morris," she says. "I haven't accused you of anything."

"No. You're just trying to make me feel guilty because I don't run like a train. What is your conception of marriage, Sophie?"

"You want my answer now, Morris? Or should I talk to a lawyer?"

"A fine answer. This is a discussion? Or an inquisition?

173

If I don't come up with the right answers, all the *yentehs* in the building will get together, pass a judgment and burn me at the stake."

"You'd be surprised," she said, "at how little anybody in the building is concerned about whether you make a fool of yourself or not. Go to sleep," she said, and turned away from me.

Good advice, go to sleep. But I needed two sleeping pills to do it.

That night I had another dream. Long ago I read a book, *Green Mansions,* probably now I would think it's kind of foolish but at the time it seemed to me very beautiful, romantic. You must know the book, from when you were a boy. There's a girl, Rima, she moves around in the forest like a bird, it's a fantasy I suppose, what the writer thought was Beauty, a dream girl, something you could never find in real life. Anyway, in my dream, it was like I was the hero in the book and I was following somebody in a jungle, sometimes it was a color I saw, sometimes a voice that I heard but I couldn't make out the words. But the voice I knew and I kept opening my mouth to say the name but nothing came out. Then, all of a sudden, there was no more jungle, I was on a pile of dirt and I was digging. Only it was with the wrong end of the shovel. I kept thinking, it's stupid, why don't I turn the shovel around and do it right, besides I didn't know why I was digging in the first place, and I was getting more and more confused and kind of angry too and I was going to stop and throw the shovel away when I felt the handle break through and the whole place where I was standing fell in. I thought good-bye Charlie, this is the end, and I couldn't remember if I'd gone to my lawyer like I intended to do, there was something in my will I wanted to

174

change. Then I was standing inside of a tomb, but it wasn't mine. There was a casket open, not a regular casket, it was made of stone like the ones you see in museums, they call them sarcophagi, but this one, instead of there being a mummy inside, there was a shaving mirror and a piece of old parchment with some funny-looking writing: "Return, return, O Shulamite, that I may look upon thee." I picked up the mirror and looked in it and there was my face, but not like now. Like when I was twenty years old. My heart was going very fast and I heard the voice again, it was saying, "Make haste, my beloved, be thou like to a young hart upon the mountain of spices." I started to run and bumped very hard against the wall of the tomb and then I woke up and my ears were ringing from the knock I just gave myself against the headboard.

Sophie woke up and said, "What's the matter?"

"I had a dream," I said, and I wanted to tell her, it was so peculiar, my heart was still knocking in my chest but she said, "Tell it to the doctor," and she went back to sleep again.

So I told it next day to the doctor. Sometimes with dreams, they get kind of rubbed out of your mind like writing on a blackboard, but this one I remembered very clear, all the details. "What does it mean?" I asked him.

"What does it mean to you?" he says.

"For God's sake," I said to him, "every time I come here you ask me if I had a dream, most of the time I can't remember, and when finally I got one, not little pieces of nothing but like a whole story, except I couldn't figure out the sense of it, you sit there and tell me I should tell *you* what it means. You are the doctor. You are supposed to tell me."

"I've explained to you that dreams have no more objective meaning than a deck of Tarot cards. I can put a construct on your dream from my knowledge of psychological symbols but that won't have any real value for you. It's your own deciphering of those symbols, what they mean in the context of your own experience, that counts. Always remember, Seidman, that what you're after is insight. That comes from within. I can help guide you to the place where the truth is but you have to see it yourself — to *want* to see it. Let's take it piece by piece. Those quotations. Can you place them?"

"They're from the Song of Songs. But they don't mean anything to me. I haven't read it in years."

"What does the shovel suggest to you?"

"Listen to me, doctor," I said. "If you say phallic symbol, I swear I will walk out of here this minute and you'll never see me again."

"Why?" he says.

"Because I heard enough of this nonsense. Everything is a phallic symbol, even my *bubba*'s umbrella. I'm sick of hearing this."

"What does jungle suggest to you?"

"I don't know. I've been reading about the Mayans in Yucatán, they found there recently some ruins in the jungle, and for sixty dollars an hour I don't have to talk about this either."

Well, it was a rotten session, I hollered on Dr. Vogel and I called him a few names and then I felt foolish and sorry and I went away thinking, what kind of an idiot am I to waste the time and the money to talk to a man who never gives me a straight answer about anything, and most of the time when I leave his office I'm more confused than ever.

This was on a Friday morning, this session, and in the afternoon Harold asked me if I would stay and close up, he wanted to leave early with Marie for the weekend at his club,

176

the weather was good for a change. I told him he could go whenever he wanted. "We arranged about this already," I said.

"I know. You said you and Mom would sit with Susie tomorrow night and Sunday, I didn't want to interfere with any other plans you might have."

I wondered, is he being considerate actually, or is he trying to get something out of me. "I've got no other plans," I said.

"Susie is all keyed up about having you all to herself tomorrow night and Sunday, two nights running."

"Just me? What about her grandmother?"

"Let's face it, pa, she prefers men. At the moment you're the big excitement in her life. You won't forget about setting the alarm," he says.

"I won't forget."

"And be sure the freight door is barred."

"I'll be sure."

"You remember we've got a new signal with Holmes — "

"Will you please go already," I said, not pianissimo. "I closed up this place for fifteen years without your instructions. I'm semi-retired, not semi-senile."

So he puts a hand on my shoulder, like you see the jockeys doing with nervous horses at the track, he gives me a smile like from a male nurse and says, "Have a good weekend, Pop." And he goes off to his club. In my time if you went away for weekends, the banks would begin to worry you're not paying enough attention to business, and they would call you in to check the credit. Nowadays, if a young executive hasn't got a membership in a club and doesn't go away Friday to Monday to play golf, they get suspicious he's juggling the books on Sunday when nobody is around, and the business is going under.

Well, this little conversation didn't put me in a very good

mood, you understand. I was in my office, standing by the window, I don't know how long I was there, I heard the voice from my dream say, "Is that really a sunset out there?"

My heart gave a knock in my throat; I turned around and I saw it was Vangie. She was standing in the doorway, wearing a light coat, no hat and no makeup on the face, and her hair hanging loose around the shoulders. "You spend a lot of time looking out of that window," she said. "What's out there that's so fascinating?"

Someplace inside my head, where Dr. Vogel has got me walking around the last couple of months, like in an attic with a flashlight, I saw the title of a book *Heart of Darkness*. By Joseph Conrad. Does anybody read his books anymore?

"What's out there? Some buildings. Some people going home. Or not going home. A lifetime. Ghosts."

"You're depressed again," she said.

"How did you guess?" I looked at my watch. "What are you doing here so late?"

"I stayed to ask some foolish questions."

"Come in," I said. "Ask."

"I just did." She walked in, her hair swinging a little against the shoulders. It's a beautiful style, if you are young and not a boy, and you've got gorgeous hair and it's not against your religion or your politics to wash and comb it sometimes.

"I have to make you a dress to go with the hair that way," I said.

"I thought you were in retirement."

"I could come out for one dress. You got any idea how beautiful you look?"

"No, tell me," she says.

"Let Ralph tell you. Wait a minute, I'll go see if there's anybody left in the shop, then I'll go down with you."

178

"There's no one," she said. "I looked."

All of a sudden I got a feeling, very strong, that this would be a different day in my life. You know how it says in the Passover service, Why is this day different from any other day? There's four reasons, maybe you know them. I could think of only one for this day, and it made a noise in my head like the traffic sound outside.

"That's a bar, isn't it?" Vangie said.

"Yes. I'm sorry, I'm so not used to drink myself, I forget it's here. Would you like something?"

"Yes, I would. Gin, if you have it."

"I got everything. I could make you a regular martini." I started to take out the bottles. "Harold put this in for me when I became Chairman of the Board. With a refrigerator and everything."

"I'll get the ice cubes," she said.

"They're right here. It's all automatic. It's not like going to chop it yourself in the icehouse but it's convenient." I didn't look at her while I was saying it and I really hated myself just then for my habit to make a joke all the time, like it was going to protect me from the Evil Eye or something. I remembered what Dr. Vogel said once about Jewish humor.

I could feel she was watching me put the ice cubes in a glass, I didn't want to see if what I said made her angry or annoyed. I poured in some gin, quite a lot, put in a couple drops of vermouth and gave her the glass. "No fruit," I said.

She tasted and said, "Mm." She picked up the bottle and looked at the label. "Plymouth," she said. I couldn't avoid her eyes anymore. "For me?" she said.

"I guess so. It's what you said to the waiter that day we had lunch with your future mother-in-law."

"I wish you wouldn't say that," she said. "Even as a

179

joke." She put down the bottle. "Did you have any trouble finding it?"

"No. I just picked up the phone and ordered it. Just in case."

"That was very nice of you," she said. "Well, here we are. Just in case."

"I hear my sister is making the engagement shower next month."

"Oh, my God. You promised you'd talk to her about that."

"I did. My sister has got a very big talent to hear only what she wants to hear. She's making the shower anyway."

"Well, I hope she enjoys it. Ralph and I won't be there. Aren't you going to have something?"

"I'll have a little Scotch. To keep you company."

"You stayed late tonight too," she said.

"I told Harold I would close up."

"I know. I heard you."

I don't know why, I thought of the dream, and again my heart gave a knock in my throat. And now the conversation went on, something like in a dream, some of it in the head altogether, without talking. Like, for instance, when she said, "No, I don't have a date," answering a question I didn't say out loud.

"I stopped in to see Edna today," she said. "On my way down from school."

"Miss Elkins told me you've stopped by quite a few times."

"They think there's still a chance the new graft will take."

"I hope so. What that poor child has been through, I wonder if it's worth it for her."

"It's worth it. Miss Elkins said they'll know by next week. If there's no sign of rejection they may send her home."

"Home," I said. "To be poisoned again. What's going to be with this world, Vangie?"

"It's going to get better. It's got to. It can't get any worse."

"And we've got to keep asking God what we could do for him, not what he could do for us."

She smiled. "I could take Edna in with me for a while."

"Wouldn't solve anything, Vangie. You can't take over her life. And there's a ward full of Ednas. But you're a fine girl to think of it. To offer it."

We didn't talk for a minute.

"Hey," she said. "Come back."

"I was thinking," I said, "maybe I should sell my Revlon stock." She didn't get it. "Suppose it would catch on," I said, "other girls would get from you an idea how nice a young girl's face could look without makeup."

"You'll turn my head, sir, saying things like that."

"You should have a date," I said. "So people could see."

"All right. Let's make one."

I felt the dream reaching out for me again, like kind of a cloud over my mind.

"I think it's time," she said, "for us to get around to something we both know has got to happen." She held out her glass. "May I have another?"

"You're sure? I put in a lot of gin before. You'll make yourself drunk."

"Fine. Being a little drunk is nice. Try it sometime."

I put more gin and a little vermouth in her glass. She took a swallow. " 'Be always drunken,' " she said. "That's Baudelaire."

"They should put him on the payroll at Seagram's."

It wasn't exactly a laugh. A nice sound, in the throat. "My first gift from a man was a book of his essays, with that passage marked."

"From the sixty-year-old French teacher?"

"Mm hm. 'Si vous ne veuillez pas — if you would not be

the martyred slave of time, be always drunken. With wine, with poetry, or with virtue.' "

"Well, at sixty, he could at least be drunk with virtue."

"Oh, man," she said. "I've given you an opening. For a bet, you're about to remind me how old you are."

"Do I have to? Vangie — "

"No," she said. She put her glass down on the bar. "I'm not going to let you talk this to death." She came over and stood in front of me. "This has been going on for weeks," she said. "I'm not shy, and I don't dream about being carried over thresholds. But it'd be nice if I didn't have to make *all* the moves."

I smelled her perfume and the dream closed in. The words I had in mind to say swam away from me. I put my arms around her and I'm ashamed to tell you what happened. No, I'm not ashamed. I'm a man, no? I held her tight, pressed up against me. I felt her trembling a little. Or maybe it was me that was trembling. After a minute, she stepped back and walked slow to the couch, taking off her dress. "You expecting any calls?" she said.

I reached to the phone and took the receiver off the hook. She was taking off her panties. "You want to help me do this?"

My heart was knocking so loud I could hardly hear her. I saw her throw the panties on a chair. They slid off and I went and picked them up and put them back on the chair. If I was a writer I would maybe say they felt like cool fire under my fingers. Must really be a difficult life, a writer, finding the words. How could you say what a piece of fruit tastes like when it's ripe and cold and you're thirsty. Or what a young girl's skin feels like. The panties were just silk. They felt like just silk. Only when I was measuring it out for dresses I never realized what silk really feels like.

182

Well, my friend, what more should I tell you? My wife and daughter, and my mother and father, and my grand-daughter, and all my Talmudic relatives back to Sodom and Gomorrah should excuse me, and all my good kosher friends should get together and pray for me on the high holidays, what I knew from the beginning was going to happen, when she walked like from out of the dream into my office, happened. It was so strong, I don't know how to describe it. There's words, of course. Overwhelming. Tidal wave. Avalanche. They're good words, they make a picture, but mostly for myself, remembering. What could they convey to anybody else about the actual experience? Looks like, for the really important things that happen to you in life, the real feelings, grief, joy, longing, loneliness, desire, there's no words actually. Labels only. Unless you felt these things yourself sometime, there's no way to tell you.

What I *could* tell you is I didn't lose control. I guess thirty years' experience counts for something, after all, but it was like the ballet was to a whole different kind of music, wild and sweet and — I give up. Maybe you could try.

The next thing I knew, it was maybe an hour later, or maybe a minute, who knows what time is, really. The window was black and lights were on in the buildings across the way. I heard her say, "Wow, that's where it's really at. God, the good earth, everything." And she put her arm across her eyes. It was a scene like from a French postcard but I didn't feel strange. What I was thinking, if you want to know, is how soon it would happen again.

"Vangie," I said, "we've got to talk."

She took away the arm from her eyes and looked at me and made a wrong conclusion. "You worried about my getting preg? I'm on the pill."

"I wasn't thinking about it," I said, "but I'm glad. There's one thing less to worry about."

183

"Listen," she says, "I'm telling you flat out, if you've got guilt feelings I don't want to hear about them."

"I've got no guilt feelings," I said. "I'm just thinking what kind of a peculiar life we've got where something wonderful happens and only trouble can come from it."

"I don't intend to have any trouble," she said. "Why should you?"

"What about Ralph?"

She gave me a look now, didn't seem too friendly. "What about Ralph?"

"Vangie, you're so modern it really doesn't bother you you've just been to bed with his uncle?"

"That's right. It doesn't bother me. Why should it?"

"A couple months ago you talked about him like you would be in love."

"That's your word, not mine."

"And beautiful boy? Those were your words."

"Maybe I've decided what I want is a beautiful man."

"Vangie, I know you and Ralph had some kind of a trial separation, he told me — "

"That's right. It took. We're making it permanent. I'm for Yucatán. He's for Angela Davis."

"Please. Don't make me more confused than I am already. You're definitely not going to marry him?"

"Definitely. I've only said so a hundred times."

"I know, but my sister Bessie says different. She'll hang herself."

"That'll be nice." She reached for her panties and bra and went into the bathroom. When she came out she said, "I gather you thought I'd bounce from here right into bed with Ralph. I'm flattered. That's really modern, man."

"Please don't be mad at me," I said. "This is a whole new experience for me. There's other things in my mind,

184

believe me. Love — excuse me for using a four-letter word — gratitude, wonder — maybe you'll accept that they are real, deep, not just establishment merchandise, sixty percent advertising. But I can't help seeing all the complications too, Vangie — "

"Okay. If you get them straightened out, come and see me sometime."

"When could it be?" I said. "In half an hour maybe?"

She's putting on her dress now and she busts out laughing. "Zip this up for me," she says, "then take me somewhere and buy me some food. Sex always makes me wildly hungry."

"I'll remember," I said. I was zipping up the dress and she turned to me and gave me a kiss, with her body pasted against me, just like in the movies.

"Listen," I said. "Take this off."

"Man," she said, "I've picked myself a real stud. Can you wait until we've had something to eat?"

"Yes. That's what I've got in mind. Go put on the Henry Kissinger dress and put your hair up and I will take you to the Three Kings for dinner."

She put her head back to look at me. "You sure?"

"You mean have I got money to pay the check?"

"I mean suppose we're seen."

"And people will suspect the worst? Like always?"

"Look," she said, "*I'm* not worried. You're the one who was talking about complications."

"You convinced me I should forget about them. Maybe this is what I really want. To be seen with a beautiful young girl, and everybody should suspect the worst. I'll find out from my analyst on Monday."

She went to the showroom to put on the dress. I called the Three Kings and made a reservation. Once upon a time,

185

to do this, I would have had to call my connection in Washington first, but now in the Nixon Era, the maître d' thought he could find me a table for two at nine-thirty, and he was even polite. I told him the dinner was a special occasion, I wanted flowers on the table, and oysters and champagne and afterward homard à l'Americain which cost me forty dollars at the Tour d'Argent in Paris to learn is broiled lobster with melted butter that I used to get at Lundy's in Sheepshead Bay for a dollar ninety-five. But in those days, it was more expensive for me than the forty dollars today. When I said I wanted, with the lobster, a bottle of Meursault '59 (this I also learned at the Tour d'Argent, for twenty-two-fifty, it was an occasion then too, Sophie's and my anniversary, and I wished I hadn't thought of it) but I could hear in the man's voice I got suddenly elected to the Beautiful People. He couldn't give me a Meursault '59 but he had a very fine Pouilly Fume '62, which for my part could have been Manischewitz '72. But I said it would do, which is what a Beautiful Person would say, I suppose, and for the main course we would have Chateaubriand, *saigneant,* with white asparagus, *vinaigrette,* and for desert a *soufflé Grand Marnier,* with a very dry champagne. I could tell he was impressed. So was I.

Then I called Sophie. The lie came easy. I remember I read somewhere, about murder, it's the first one that's hard to do, after that, comes easier, with each one.

In the restaurant, the maître d' did his twenty-dollar *kazatski* taking us to the table and if what I wanted was attention, I got it. The stares didn't make me feel good, or proud. Not bad either. Not ashamed, not guilty. Maybe I've lived not according to my real nature all these years. Maybe I'm just another Larry, with a little knowledge of the Talmud.

186

When the waiter came I said, "Bring the lady a very dry martini, Plymouth gin, in an old fashioned glass, with ice, no fruit. Scotch for me, with soda. And never mind the menu, I ordered already."

The waiter went away and Vangie said, "Why did you do that?"

"What?"

"Order my dinner."

"I don't know. I suppose I thought you would like me to."

"I don't. I don't want people taking over my life."

"You want to make a Women's Lib manifesto over a dinner?"

"That's not one of your better jokes. I want to eat what I feel like eating, not what *you* order."

"Vangie, you'll eat whatever you want. Don't make a *tsimmes* about nothing."

The waiter came with the drinks.

"*Le chayim,*" I said.

She didn't say anything, just drank the martini. Another waiter came with champagne in a bucket and a third waiter with oysters.

"Take them away," I said. "And cancel the rest of the order. I'll tell you later what the lady wants for dinner."

The waiter starts to take away the oysters and she says, "Leave them, please. And don't cancel the rest of the dinner, we'll have it as ordered."

"Yes, *moddom,*" he said and went away backward, like in the movies. Everything tonight was like in the movies. Except the male star got into the film by mistake.

She sat looking down at the oysters with the little fork in her hand. "Vangie," I said, "please don't eat them on my account. Tell me what you want and I'll order it for you."

"I've got exactly what I want," she said, and I heard her

187

voice was a little funny, wobbly. "I'm mad for oysters. I *lust* for them when they're out of season." She looks up at me now and I see there's tears in her eyes. "You're right," she said. "It's a damn peculiar world where something wonderful happens and all it can do is louse up your life."

"Not all," I said. "I want to wait till tomorrow with the complications. If we're in trouble it's too late to do anything about it. I already lied to my wife, that I'm going to be in a Turkish Bath."

She put her hand out and put it on mine. "What's *tsimmes*," she said.

"It's a traditional Jewish dish. Made with carrots and prunes and sweet potatoes and honey."

"Seems like Jews had some idea about natural foods too."

"Then explain me why they've got the worst digestions in the world?"

"Because they sit around squeezing the life out of every proposition, instead of getting out and taking some healthful exercise."

"Please. Not golf."

"Okay. Not golf. Lacrosse? Ice hockey?"

"Larry says the best exercise is indoors."

"Please don't quote Larry to me. Making a *tsimmes.* Making a big deal, right?"

"Something like it. You got the general idea."

"Don't make a *tsimmes*. Don't get uptight."

"I think so. What's uptight?"

"Making a *tsimmes*."

We laughed. It was foolish, but wonderful. "You want another martini?" I said.

"Let's have the champagne. They say it's the friend of lovers."

"You mean people who are in love? You got to be more

specific, Vangie." She gave me a look and I said, "All right. I heard the same thing about oysters."

"The friend of lovers? Where'd you hear that?"

"From Larry. I'll take his word for it. A man in my position needs all the friends he can get."

She laughed again, that delicious sound, then she ate like a horse. A small horse.

You know how I remember things. I remember everything about that night. Lucky they're only good memories, they could spoil my life. Like Heathcliff. Heathcliff and Cathy on Central Park West? 'Heathcliff, fill my arms with lox and bagels.' It's a funny idea.

There's a couple of special things. I was *dremmling* a little, you know, with the eyes open and I heard her say, "Tell me."

I turned to look at her.

"You were far away," she said.

"Yes. Another world. Another life."

"You too? Where were you?"

"The gallery at Carnegie Hall."

"Oh. I thought maybe it was Carthage. Or along the Nile — "

"You really believe in that stuff, Vangie."

"I didn't pick archaeology as my major by accident. What about the gallery at Carnegie?"

"I went to hear Jascha Heifetz, the first time. He played Bruch's Concerto. The G minor one."

"Very schmaltzy."

"Maybe. To me it was the most beautiful thing I ever heard in my life. Tell me, Vangie, why is it whenever I hear something beautiful, or see something beautiful, I feel like crying."

"Because you're Jewish."

"You don't feel this way?"

"Oh yes. But I'm Jewish too."

"When did you decide?"

"I think it was about five thousand years ago. In Egypt."

"You were making potato pancakes for somebody then too?"

She laughed, then she said, "Don't joke about reincarnation. I want to come back."

"Not me," I said. "I would be a dress manufacturer all over again. Once is enough."

"No," she said. "You'd be a poet. Or a musician."

"Or maybe a waiter in a Jewish restaurant in New Peking on the Hudson. Because we didn't stop them after all in Vietnam."

"Are you serious?" she said, moving a little away from me.

"Come back," I said. "Is it important to you I should be a liberal?"

"I want to know who you voted for for President last time," she said. "Right now."

"You are violating my Constitutional rights. We got something called the secret ballot. Just because I am in bed with you, do I have to agree with your politics? Is this reasonable, Vangie? After all the *shmoos* you gave me about people not moving in on each other. Taking over their *nishomehs?*"

"What's *nishomehs?*"

"Souls."

"I'm not appropriating your *nishomeh*," she said. I want to know who you voted for. It's your right not to tell me. And it's my right to tell you to go home to your nest of reactionaries on Central Park West."

"Have you got a wrong number! If you find a reactionary on Central Park West, he is probably working for the C.I.A. making up those dossiers on the residents."

"Are you going to tell me?"

"You are destroying my individuality. But I'll tell you this much. It wasn't Nixon. Okay?"

"Okay for now. I want to know more of what you think about Vietnam."

"How did we get to Vietnam? I was talking about the first time I heard Jascha Heifetz."

"Heifetz hasn't given concerts in years. When was this?"

"A long time ago. Maybe thirty-five years. Does it make you feel funny that you've been balling with a man who was listening to Heifetz ten years before you were born?"

"Say making love. Balling doesn't sound right, coming from you."

"Why? It's just a word."

"I know. But it doesn't sound right."

"Doesn't sound right to me coming from you either, if you want to know."

"All right. I won't say it anymore. I'll say making love."

"Tell the truth, Vangie, isn't it nicer? The sound? Let's make love?"

"Yes," she said. "Let's make love."

"You're testing?" I said. "Or you're inviting me."

"You feel up to it?"

"I could try."

I was up to it, my friend. I wouldn't have believed what I was up to that night.

One other thing. Very special. I remember there was light in the room, beige with some ink mixed in. I was groggy but inside wide awake, like there was full light shining on me from somewhere and I saw her, reaching up her arms to stretch. I don't know why it looked to me like something in a ballet, so beautiful — and I thought, something is gone, something I will never have again, and it gave me such a twist inside I thought maybe I'm going to have a heart attack now, the one I've been secretly wishing for all these weeks, months, a fine thing, Jewish dress manufacturer taken from model's apartment, dead on arrival at Mount Sinai.

She turned to me. "I thought you were sleeping."

"No. I got lots of time to sleep. What were you thinking just now?"

"Guess."

"I can't. The radar stopped working a couple of hours ago."

"I was thinking I'm going to have all the sex I need or want in my life," she said. "But what am I going to do for talk, when this is over? Who's going to say *yontevdik* and *draydle* and *tsimmes* and all the other funny, lovely words? Who's going to make me laugh, the way you do, when half the time I'm not sure that what I really want to do isn't to cry?"

You know, it's not all bad, technology. It's nice somebody invented records and hi-fi so I'll be able to sit and listen to Bruch's Concerto, with Jascha Heifetz, and remember.

"Doctor," I said. "I've been cheating on my wife."

I wait for him to say something. Naturally, nothing.

"Could you say something," I said. "Just to give me a clue you're not a statue sitting there, you're really alive and you heard what I said."

"I heard you," he says. "I'm waiting for you to continue."

"You got no comment? I didn't say it's raining outside. I said I've been cheating on my wife."

"What would you like me to say?"

"Anything. 'What else is new?' for instance."

"This isn't new, Seidman. Or rather it's not news. I've been expecting it."

"Why didn't you tell me?"

"I'm not here to tell you. You're here to tell me."

"You expect me to say I feel guilty, I suppose."

"I expect you to tell me how you feel about it."

"I feel fine about it."

"You used the word cheating. That implies guilt. Do you feel fine and guilty? Or guilty and fine?"

"You think you got me trapped in some kind of a hypocrisy. Well, happens I feel both. Fine and guilty."

"Can you be a little more explicit?"

"Yes. I feel like I'm the luckiest man alive. Like I dropped twenty years from my age. Like the world suddenly got a bath in moonbeams and I'm seeing it for the first time. You want me to say I feel also like a sneak and a cheat. All right, I do. But why, doctor? What contract did I make to sign away the rights to my soul. Why should I feel guilty? What kind of rotten deal is it to be saddled with this kind of morality?"

"Seidman, let me quote from your friend Shakespeare. 'Nothing is good or bad but thinking makes it so.' You have to try to understand *why* you feel this way."

"I *don't* understand. I'll never understand."

"Or you don't want to understand?"

I didn't say anything. He didn't say anything.

"What was the occasion of your cheating, as you put it," he says finally.

"The occasion was three weeks ago Friday, in my office and every occasion I could beg, borrow or steal since."

"You skipped some sessions during that time. But you've also had a few. Why didn't you mention this before?"

"That's a good question, doctor. I guess, some way, in my mind, you are my judge — "

"Your father, perhaps?"

"Maybe my father."

193

"And what? You didn't want to upset your father? Get a lecture on morality? Be disowned? What?"

"I don't know. I had a secret. A wonderful secret. Like a jewel shining inside my head. I didn't want to say anything about it."

"Why?"

"Maybe because to talk about it would spoil it some way."

"Why?"

"I don't know. Maybe you could tell me."

"I'll tell you one thing. You're not fencing with me today. That's a welcome change. What are you thinking now?"

"You'll say I'm back to fencing."

"Risk it."

"There's a poem by an English writer, I forget his name; maybe you heard it. 'Say I'm weary, say I'm sad, say that health and wealth have missed me, say I'm growing old but add, Jenny kissed me.' That's what I was thinking."

"The name is Vangie, of course. Jenny is your daughter's name."

"Yes. And if I was a poet instead of a dress manufacturer, I would have written that down, something like it, and sent it to you, and saved myself a visit. But if I was a poet instead of a dress manufacturer I guess I wouldn't have come to you in the first place."

"I have a poet among my patients, of considerable reputation. He comes to see me four times a week."

"I'm glad to hear he makes that kind of money."

"His parents have the money. He writes beautiful poetry and he's a very sick man. I'm not at all sure I can help him."

I didn't say anything. What's to say? All my life I had the idea that to be a poet is to be a king, a god.

"Are you in love with this girl?" the doctor asks me now.

"I'm going to answer you with a question, doctor. And I

194

am not playing games, believe me. What is love? What do you mean, in love?"

He thinks for a long minute. "You're right to question me, Seidman. You've come a long way."

There was like a hand inside my throat, squeezing.

"What *are* your feelings about this girl?" he said.

"I don't know how to answer. She's like a daughter. She's like a woman with all the tenderness and all the wisdom in the world. She's like my wife when we were young. I don't mean she looks like her. But the same feeling that I've got the most beautiful girl in the world in my arms and I'm pushing up the sky with my head — or my behind — lucky she can't hear me saying this, she would throw something at me."

"This is the first time you've — er — well, strayed, in your marriage?"

"Yes. Well, no. Actually the second time. There was a Japanese girl a few years ago — but nothing happened. It's another story entirely. I'll tell you something, doctor, my wife doesn't need to feel insulted I've been tempted by just anybody in a skirt, or a kimono."

"What happened then?"

"I told you, nothing. In the middle of everything, I thought about my daughter and my obligations, and my image — Seidman, the righteous man — and it was finished. Some *shnook*. And you can see, I'm still the same *shnook*. Only a little closer to the grave. Maybe I got some courage from this, I was more reckless, or the girl understood better — I don't know."

"What do you think this girl feels about you?"

"Excuse me, doctor, but I think I could see the direction in which you are going. I'll save time. I don't give her money."

195

"You're convinced you've got some kind of radar, aren't you, Seidman?"

"Was I wrong?"

"Yes. What *do* you give her?"

"Talk, believe it or not. This is what she values. I think why she was attracted to me in the first place is I made her laugh."

"I take it you have no problems with her in bed."

"All my good friends should have such problems. There's something else."

"Yes? Why are you hesitating?"

"I know you want me to speak what's in my mind. Net. T.O.T. But I don't want you should think I'm a sentimental slob."

"I doubt there's anything you could say that would make me think that."

"Well, you want to know what I think was for her the most important thing? She's got a woman's heart, a real woman, a beautiful thing in a world that is pretty ugly. She thought I needed her. This is for her the big thing, that makes for her the great sex, everything."

"I see. Kind of a sexual social service."

"*You're* making the jokes now? Fine thing. It's still my money, don't forget."

"You're not likely to let me forget. Look, aside from the talk and making her laugh and needing her — or putting all those together, has it occurred to you that this indefinable thing we call love — that she may be in love with you?"

"No, it hasn't occurred to me. And I don't want it should occur to me. Or to her. I am more than twice her age, she's got a wonderful life ahead of her, I don't want to mix it up. And I don't want what's left of my life to be mixed up either, chasing a fantasy in a forest."

196

"I don't get the allusion."

"Rima, the bird girl. My youth."

"Is she going away?"

"Yes. To Mexico. She is going to work for her master's degree in archaeology."

"You're not tempted to go with her?"

"Tempted? Oh, man, am I tempted. But I told you, I don't want to mix up her life. *My* life? What's left? I'm married, I would like to stay married."

"Have you told your wife about this affair?"

"No. Should I?"

"Yes," he says. "I think you should."

"Doctor, you realize what you just said? This is a revolution."

"Your analysis is about over, Seidman. What I just told you, I told you as a friend, who's come to know you."

"Why do you think it's a good idea, to tell my wife? You don't believe what a wife doesn't know wouldn't hurt her?"

"I believe the only kind of relationship that you'd regard as worth having is an honest one. There's a risk. But that's what I believe."

It was a nice thing to hear from a man I spent nearly three months needling the life out of him.

Harold came into my office in the afternoon to tell me Vangie is leaving.

"I know," I said.

"She'll be hard to replace," he said.

"You've got three models left," I said. "They could do the work until the season really starts. Then if you need another girl, you could get one."

"I'll miss her," he said. Then after a minute, "I guess you will too."

"Yes," I said. "She's a very nice girl. Makes a very nice impression on people."

He looked at me for a minute. Then he said, "I think she's a very nice girl too, Pa. I want you to know that."

He started to walk to the door. "Harold," I said. He turned around. "What do you think of marriage?"

He didn't answer right away. "Depends," he said. "Your marriage or mine?" He gives me a little smile.

"I mean, in general, marriage."

"I don't know what to say. A sacrament. The tie that binds. A necessary prelude to divorce. I don't know. Is this a survey, Pa? Or something personal?"

"How about, it's a long-term contract for mutual suicide."

"Sounds like someone trying to be deep."

"It's from a model that you know."

"Vangie?"

"Yes. She was serious. Or, anyway, she thought she was serious. She could change her mind, I suppose."

"Well, the kids have gone past me," he said. "Of course, she's not a kid either."

"But to you it's a good thing? Marriage?"

"If you mean do I think it would have been a good thing for her to marry Ralph, no. I don't think that would have lasted a year."

"Why do you say that?"

"Just a feeling I have. Mostly on account of Ralph. He's a nice kid, actually. But he's going to be the same nice kid when he's forty. Maybe I'm doing him an injustice but that's the feeling I've got about him."

"Funny. It's almost the identical thing Vangie said. But for you it's worked out fine? Marriage?"

"Yes. Overall."

"Suppose you wouldn't have been married to Marie."

"I've supposed that, on occasion. We've had quarrels. And I've walked out."

"You think it's marriage made you come back."

"Who knows? Maybe if we weren't married, I'd have stayed away too long, and by the time I decided to come back it might have been too late."

"Is it worth much, then, if this is all that holds two people together?"

"Yes, I think it is. If we're going to be real serious about it, I don't think we're much beyond the crawling stage in the evolutionary scale. I mean, psychologically. Emotionally. Ethically. I think we need restraints, a framework of discipline, to keep from getting ourselves hopelessly messed up. I think the kids are going to find that out. Some of them, too late."

"Harold, if I would have said this to you twelve years ago, you'd have called me a Nazi."

"I'd never have called you a Nazi. I'd have disagreed with you."

"Enough to move away from the house."

"Seems I didn't move very far." He gave me again a smile and I got a remembrance suddenly of a small boy looking up at me in a pet shop, when we found a dog he fell in love with. Remember? Hercules?

"What have you got to quarrel about, you and Marie?" I said. "This is the first I've heard of it."

"Oh, the usual stuff," he said. "She thinks I spend too much time in the shop. Delegate authority. That's the phrase. She read in a book somewhere that all the big executives know how to delegate authority."

"She wants you home more. This should make you feel good. Not angry."

"Pa, I'm sure you've been through this. It's fine they

want you home but you'd like some understanding of what's involved in running a business. Right?"

"You want me to take back some of the responsibility? I could handle the piece goods, if you want."

"No. Please. Remember what you used to drum into my head from my Hebrew lessons? 'Whatsoever falleth to thy hand to do, do it with thy might.' "

"I remember. All right. I wouldn't butt in."

He gave me a smile, started to go, then stopped. "There was a girl a while back, Pa. Didn't amount to anything actually. But it tore things up for us pretty good for a while."

I had a big hunger just then to give him a hug but how do you do this with a thirty-two-year-old man, who's married to a Gentile?

"We ought to have a talk sometime," he said. "A real one. Like in the old days."

"Fine," I said. "We'll take a long lunch some day. I would like it. But not just now."

"Sometimes it helps to get things off your chest."

"What do you think has been going on with the analyst?"

"Oh yes. I forgot." He goes to the door and again he stops. "Pa, you don't mind if I ask you something? You're not planning anything drastic, are you?"

"For instance."

"Getting a divorce?"

"I don't want it, Harold. But there's two people involved. I don't know what your mother will want."

"Does she know what's been going on?"

"I couldn't tell you. I don't think so. After all, for thirty-three years I didn't give her much reason not to trust me. Anyway, tonight she'll know."

"You're going to tell her?"

"Yes."

"Why? You'll only hurt her. Women don't understand these things."

"I can't help it, Harold. I don't want to live like a sneak."

"But the girl's going away — "

"Harold, her plane leaves from Kennedy ten o'clock tomorrow morning. How do I know when it will take off from in here?"

She was in her dressing room, at the mirror, brushing her hair. She is still a beautiful woman, my Sophie. It hit me very hard that moment that what I was going to say to her now, I could lose her.

"Sophie, I've got something to tell you."

She didn't say anything. I didn't think it would be easy, before. But I didn't think it would be this hard.

I said, "Sophie, I've been having an affair."

"I know," she said.

Of all the things I could have imagined she would say, this was the last.

"How do you know?"

"Because I know."

"So you're not surprised."

"Why should I be? You're a goat, like every other man."

"You're not angry?"

"I told you you were free to do whatever you felt you needed to do to express yourself. You don't owe me any explanations or apologies or excuses."

"The way you say express yourself, I could be a tube of toothpaste, or a return package to Altman's."

Again she doesn't say anything, just keeps on brushing her hair.

"Sophie, will you stop brushing your hair, for God's sake. I can't talk to the back of your head."

"You told me you've been having an affair. All right, you've been having an affair. Period."

"What do you mean, period. Stop brushing your hair already. I want to talk to you. Turn around."

She turns around. "Sixty-eight," she says.

"What sixty-eight?"

"It's not sex," she says. "I brushed sixty-eight times. I've got thirty-two more to go. Remind me."

"Sophie, you're furious with me."

"That's what you want me to be, isn't it? I'm not furious."

"Then what are you? Tell me."

"I don't know. Sleepy."

"Sophie, I'm going to ask you something and I want a straight answer."

"If you're going to ask if I also had an affair, the answer is no. Not lately."

"This is not what I want to ask you." Then I said, "What do you mean not lately?"

"I mean not lately. Can I resume brushing my hair, my lord? I want to get to bed."

"Sophie, I want a straight answer. Did you encourage me to have an affair, or didn't you?"

"Maybe I did. But I didn't encourage you to come and tell me about it."

"You'd rather I went around feeling like a sneak."

"Right now, Morris, I'm not interested in how you feel. I'm interested in how I feel."

"How do you feel? Tell me."

"A little tired. A little old."

"Sophie." I took a step toward her and she lifted the brush.

"Stay away from me, Morris. I'm warning you."

I wanted to tell her how beautiful she looked to me that minute, how it squeezed my heart to know how much I cared for her, how much I wanted never to hurt her. But I knew she would take it wrong, like it was a cheap bid for forgiveness.

She was brushing her hair again. "Are you planning to continue this relationship?" she said.

I took a deep breath. Then I said, "Sophie, I don't know how you will take this, but the question is out of order."

She turned her head and gave me a look, I can't describe it. Maybe if she saw a mouse running across the room carrying a placard, Excelsior, maybe this would be the kind of expression.

"Just because I married you thirty-three years ago," I said, "does not give you proprietary rights in my personal life. One of the problems in our society — "

"Shut up," she said and threw down the brush so it knocked over some of the bottles. "Just shut up. If you're getting ready to ask me to divorce you, the answer is yes. Whenever you want. But don't make me any cockamamie declarations of independence. I don't have to listen to that bullshit."

Honest to God, she said it. I didn't know whether to laugh, or cry, or hit my head against the wall. "Sophie, I didn't expect from you this kind of language."

"Fine," she says. "This will end up with me apologizing to you for my language. Go away, Morris. Please. Sleep in the guest room. Or go back and sleep with your mistress."

"You are not going to shut me up, Sophie," I said. "This has got to be talked out between us, once and for all. First of all, I don't know what you want, but I don't want a divorce."

"Then what?" she said. "You want to keep up with this affair until you fall down from a coronary and then I should nurse you back to health, like a loving and forgiving wife. Thank you very much. No."

"There is not going to be any more affair," I said. "What

I am talking about now is a matter of principle. Women are going around now *hocking a tchynik* about how unfair they are treated by men, and marriage is an institution that has got men locked up in prison."

I don't think she even heard what I said. "All that has to happen now," she said, she was brushing her hair now like it got tangled, "is for her to tell Ralphie. He'll kill you."

How do you like that? Not only she knows, but she knows who. What kind of service do they subscribe to? Or is there for real some kind of ESP?

"He won't kill me," I said. "I'm not so easy to kill, and besides it's finished with her and Ralphie."

She looked up at me. "She's not going to marry him?"

"No. I told you, it's finished."

"What's going to be with the shower Bessie is making?"

"This is what's worrying you now? You could make Care packages of the chopped liver and send them to Pakistan. What is the matter with you, Sophie? What kind of question — ?"

"I'll ask you another one. Is she going to marry *you* maybe?"

"You haven't been listening to me at all? I told you. It's over. She's going to Yucatán to dig."

"I don't believe it. She's going to stay here and dig. I'll tell you nicely, Morris. Not my half. Unless you want a real scandal."

"Sophie, I'm telling you she's going away. It's over. Finished."

"So?" She swings around now and I see there's sparks coming from her eyes. "You want to cry a little maybe? On my shoulder?"

"No," I said. "I want to make love to you." And a funny thing. I really did. Suddenly. Very strong.

*

Well, I wouldn't drag it out. We made love and afterward she said, "I must be a pervert. Next thing I'll be inviting someone into bed with us."

"Just so it's not a Ph.D."

"Don't think he hasn't been trying. Maybe I should have an affair with him?"

"Just to even up the score?"

"I'm a little curious. Maybe I've been missing something."

"You got me in a funny position, Sophie. If you're serious, I could only tell you you've got a right to do what you want."

"But you wouldn't like it."

"I would hate it. But people got to learn. We don't own each other."

"It's a little late in life for us, Morris."

"Dr. Vogel says if you got only one day left, you should use it to learn something, especially how to act like a human being, not a predator or a sheep."

"You're finished with him?"

"Yes. I'm dismissed. He's a good man, Sophie. I learned a lot from him."

After a minute she says, "How was it with her?"

"You want to talk about this, Sophie? I don't think we should."

"I want to talk about it," she said.

"You're sure?"

"Yes. Suddenly you're getting reticent? It's too precious a memory — "

"All right," I said. "I'm not going to lie to you. It was wonderful."

"You have to tell me? You're going to tell me now how many times, and how she went out of her mind — "

"I'm going to tell you what I told you. It was wonderful.

For a few weeks. But I'll be fifty-six next month and she's twenty-two and I'm glad it happened, I'm grateful to her, I'm glad for the way it made me feel, but I'm glad she's going away. Everything I'm telling you is the truth."

"All right," she said. "I believe you. You'll miss her, I suppose."

"Yes." She waited as if she expected me to say more. There was more to say but where were the words?

After a while she said, "You don't think it's spoiled everything for us?"

"Sophie, wasn't it spoiled before? When I was going around like an old fogy, only feeling sorry for myself? Always depressed, because I was in a rage actually, because I realized more than two thirds of my life is gone and I'm not Heifetz, and I'm not Shakespeare, I'm only a dress manufacturer with a double A rating in Dun and Bradstreet. This girl brought me back to myself, Sophie. All right, I got some help from the analyst too. I feel like a man again, not an old Jew. Retired. I want to do things. I want to go to Israel maybe, and plant trees. Start up a business there, I don't know, something. Besides you just had a sample. Do you think it's spoiled?"

"I think I'm sleepy now. But maybe I'll wake up later. Does that scare you?"

"Try," I said. "A person never knows his real capacities until he tries."

I got a letter today from Vangie.

DEAR MAN: A bulletin from your Constant Admirer. Yucatán isn't Eden but it'll do for this fledgling archaeologist. You have to be a little cracked to begin with to get involved in this stuff. There's no money, and no applause; you're just a kind of ghoulish kid playing with old bones, or to put a better face on it, an architect of shadows, rebuilding the past, which is just one big shadow, actually. But passion is passion, it can't be explained rationally, as you must know from talking to the golfers at your club.

I get enough to eat. Gourmet food it's not, as you would say. The basic culinary idea seems to be, when in doubt add more green chile and tabasco. Plymouth gin is a forlorn memory (don't try to send me any, it'll never reach me) but margaritas are an acceptable replacement for martinis, if you throw in Palenque and occasional side trips to Chichén-Itzá and Uxmal.

I'm keeping company. He's on leave from Yale University to find some clue to the Mayan writings, which is a pleasantly mind-cracking way to spend your time, he says, if you're hipped on hieroglyphics. You'd like him, I think. He's older than you are, forty-one, but young in spirit and not as goy-ish as he might be, since he looks very much like Trevor Howard. You'll be pleased to know I've given up childish ways and stopped putting a tuning fork to sex to find out if it's hitting E above high C. That's a kind of romantic crap too, just as phony as the music-in-my-feet jazz. So the cadenza didn't bring the house down last time. So you didn't feel the earth move. So?

There's a village not far from the dig where we go to shop and rubberneck and drink, at the cantina. It probably hasn't changed much in the past couple of hundred years. The men are beautiful to look at, in their gleamy white clothes and teeth; they're reserved, courteous, great at minding their own business. Their kids never come running up to holler, Daddy, look only one cavity; they'd probably get their heads broken and besides, they don't have any cavities at all, the legend is it's the chile that does it. (Fends off polio too, they say.)

It's hard to believe that just a few centuries ago, these people were throwing young girls into wells as offerings to their gods. At that, the Mayans seem to have been less pious in their religious observances than their Aztec cousins to the north, who tore the skin off their captives, preferably female, as chasubles for their priests, or devotional offerings to their war god. (Huitzilipochtli by name. That's one to twist around your tongue when you've got a mouthful of re-fried beans.) I've got a figure of him that I keep around, to remind me how close we live to horror. (Those Vietnam body counts that came just before the commercials for freeze-dried coffee.) Huitzi is beautiful, plastically speaking, and it rocks the mind to think of the screams that went into the worshiping of him. We're fearfully and wonderfully made, for a fact. To need a Moloch, devourer of children, an Allah summoning his faithful for a *jehad* to slay the infidel, a Jehovah sending his servant Joshua into Jericho to 'utterly destroy' — men, women, young, old, not forgetting oxen, sheep and asses — it's a nice touch that the only one who got out alive was a harlot. Is there a message here for the chaste that's been overlooked these many years?

But it gives one to think, all this endless carnage in the name of something holy or other. Just when did the terrible brainstorm hit the cowering half-beast during the intervals between Ice Ages — the idea of a God, who's supposed to give a damn, and be placated, and have his feet washed in blood regularly?

I haven't checked lately to see if I'm happy. If happiness is doing your thing — I can see you wince. All right, I'll start over; if happiness is doing what you like best to do, I'm doing it and I'm happy. Each day on the dig brings its parcel of quiet excitement — in the worth-words of that nineteenth century *noodnick,* Wordsworth, its intimations of immortality. (I treasure them; I've told you, in spite of all the crap, I want to come back.)

My new friend wants to get married. (Where does the fiction come from that it's women who want to get married?) Sometimes I weaken and start to think about babies and such and the battle that goes on inside gets rough. So far I've managed to prevail against that built-in booby trap. But I'm not at all sure how my resolution will hold up when that inescapable number "thirty" begins to play around the fringes of my consciousness.

Every once in a while, too, I'm grabbed by the notion of flying up to New York for a few days to see you, or asking you to fly down here for a visit. It passes, and sweet reason takes over. I'll tell you what, I'm not going to fight City Hall. But next time around, please check my whereabouts before getting yourself tied up with a wife and grandchildren and all. If making inquiries for Vangie doesn't get results, try asking for a girl who doesn't look so *yontevdik* because she hasn't had a good laugh for a few centuries and she's pining for some meaningful *shmoos*.

We rapped a lot about love, didn't we. Did we ever decide anything? Other than that I conceded that "making love" sounds better than balling. Despite that rotten rooster from my childhood. I keep thinking about it. How about: Love is never having to say you're sorry — unless you've done something to be sorry for, and then you damn well ought to have the grace and the guts to say so, and bring flowers or something.

Stay well, please.

YOUR VANGIE

∽ ∽ ∽

We went to sit for my granddaughter Susie last night. I have to tell you about this little girl. You've heard probably from parents a remark that a certain child is specially precious to them because they almost lost her. We are not the parents but Susie is extra special precious to us because we lived through that time with Harold and Marie.

She was six and a half pounds when she was born and a week later she weighed five and a half. Before they found out what was wrong with her she was down to practically nothing; she was like a skinny chicken when they took her to the operating room to cut out an intestinal block that was stopping her from getting any nourishment. Afterward they put her in an incubator, they kept her there nearly three months, with all kinds of tubes stuck in her. A few times a day someone, a nurse, or her mother, or Sophie would take turns holding her for a few minutes outside the incubator, so she could feel the contact with a living person. You see, it's not enough for the little creatures to have protein and glucose and so on, they've got to feel love long before they could know or say the word, so they could grow up into people who don't know what the word means.

Susie is six now, a beautiful child, takes after her mother, we were worried the time she wasn't getting any sustenance, maybe her brain would be affected. But she is normal, more than normal, she's got the mental age of a child of eight, not six. There's left from the whole experience only a little hesitation in the speech that makes her only more adorable.

This evening I brought her a book about a horse, Black Beauty, she is crazy about horses. I'm waiting for the time I could bring her a real horse, a pony, instead of a book.

"Will you read it to me?" she said.

"I thought you would read it to me, Susie."

"No, you read it to me."

210

"How about we should read it to each other."

"All right. But you start."

So I started to read and all of a sudden she sat up in her bed and twisted her arms around my neck. "I love you, Grandpa," she said. Her arms are still a little skinny from the time when she was in the Intensive Care, they had to put splints on them so she wouldn't break them, moving around, they were like chicken bones.

"What's love, Susie?" I asked her.

"I don't know."

"Then why do you say you love me?"

"Because I do."

"Because I bring you presents?"

"No."

"Because I read to you? And tell you stories?"

"No."

"Then why?"

She thought for a minute, the beautiful little *shicksah* face very serious. Then she said, "Because you're funny."

Well, my writer friend, it's a tough world; my analyst, I should say my doctor friend, he is not on my payroll anymore, we have lunch sometimes and I give him free advice about his problems at home. Seriously, I'll tell you a funny development. He plays the cello, about the same virtuoso class as me with the violin, we started to get together one evening a week, my Jenny took a good pill and she stays home that night to play with us the piano part for trios, easy ones, Haydn and so on, what it sounds like to the neighbors I couldn't tell you but we are making music and it's somehow a satisfying feeling.

But what I started out to say about Vogel is I got something from him that was worth all the time and money. It was during one of the sessions, I was carrying on about my wasted life, my depression and so on, and he said to me — for once I heard an irritation in his voice, finally I achieved to get him fed up with me — he said, "Seidman, did you ever hear of Helen Keller?"

I told him yes, she was the fantastic woman who became a great educator, without being able to see or hear.

"Maybe you think," Vogel said, "you're entitled to a Congressional citation because you got an education under difficult circumstances; maybe you think — for all your self-deprecation — that you should have a statue erected in your honor in Herald Square? You're full of self-pity, you're running over with it. Well, let me tell you something. If you get up in the morning and you can walk and see and hear, and you go out in the street and nobody shoots you or knocks you down or mugs you, you've got from the world all you've a right to expect. Pull yourself together for God's sake, and realize how much more you've got than most people, how much more you've accomplished, and stop whining."

"Well," I said, "I'm glad to find out finally I'm not locked up here with a computer. You're disgusted with me. We've got something in common. *I'm* disgusted with me. Maybe now we'll get somewhere."

"We'll get nowhere," he said, "if I let you get under my skin. You've been trying to do that from the beginning and you've succeeded. For what it's worth to you, congratulations. Now, let's get back to business."

A very good man. I could recommend him if you've got a problem. (I could just hear you say, "I'll send him my producer, he's my problem.")

Anyway, what Vogel said to me that time is something I'll never forget. Who says we've got a right to expect anything from the world? From the moon and the stars and the mountains? Who says we're supposed to be happy? If your six-year-

212

old granddaughter puts her arms around your neck and says she loves you because you're funny, if a woman who's lived with you nearly a lifetime could still find some affection for you in her heart, if a girl born five thousand years ago in Egypt, who doesn't know what love means, but holds it out to you anyway, like a hand to someone drowning, you've got to be a fool, worse than a fool, to keep looking for definitions, what love is. In your heart you know what it is. It's from God, my friend, whoever he is or wherever, and if you got a chance, be thankful and grab it, whatever is the reason, whatever it costs, it's a bargain.